S0-ATI-131

In Her, Through Her!

The Great Mother was all life, all Change, and within Her
all knowledge, all rules were meant to be transformed.
Now they are being broken, snapped like dry twigs,
and Talker, aged and crafty, ignited by the new emotions
of greed and ambition, feeds the flame of Change to
its worse end, scheming to take power from the wise matriarchs,
and wield it for himself.
Old Manka the Taken, healer and shaman,
sees the lies and violence spread through the Kindred. But she is old
and her power declines. It is two newly-Taken ones, a girl and a boy
barely out of childhood, who hold the key to healing
the evil which has arisen.
But first, to gather their powers
they must Wander. . . .

FIRES of the
KINDRED

ROBIN SKELTON

FIRES of THE KINDRED

Porcépic Books

Victoria • Toronto

Copyright 1987 by Robin Skelton

All rights reserved.

No part of this book may be reproduced or transmitted in any form by any means, electronic or mechanical, including photo-copying, recording or any information storage, retrieval, and transmission systems now known or to be invented, without per-mission in writing from the publisher, except by a reviewer who may quote brief passages in a review.

This edition is published by Press Porcépic Ltd., 235-560 Johnson St., Victoria, B.C. V8W 3C6, with the assistance of the Canada Council.

Canadian Cataloguing in Publication Data

Skelton, Robin, 1925 -
    Fires of the Kindred

    ISBN 0-88878-271-3

    I. Title
    PS8537.K44F5 1987   C813'.54   C87-091306-9
    PR9199.3.S54F5 1987

59,200

to

Sean Virgo

CAMROSE LUTHERAN COLLEGE
LIBRARY

ONE

It was in the year of the briar that he finished making the head. They called it the year of the briar because that Spring the brown withered thongs had snaked green lengths over the thorns and stones in a fashion no one had known before.

It was not a thing of worship or to let blood for; it was simply the solid version of thought, a stone thinking, a stone knowing. It took three men to get it to the Gathering Place and put it there, granite rasping the finger-palps, at every stumble the great eyes seeming to watch, the mouth appearing to smile. "Her face," they said, "Her face," and they put bracken round it, and he was pleased as a Maker is always pleased when his heart is made whole.

And so it was then a matter of where to put it, and when, for the when is also the where as places change through time. One said "By the crooked thorn," and one said "In the dip of the hill by the heather," but the Chooser said that it should be set in the wall about the place the giftings were kept, for the giftings were Hers and every part of them was a gift from Her—the flesh for meat, the skins for bladders, the bones for scrapers and diggers, even the hairs to twist together—and that it should be set there at dawn.

So there the head was set and in that year of the briar the brambles raked round up and through the crevices of the wall and the bracken shoved its fronds up tall and by high summer the head peered through a mask of bracken and bramble at the lank lad herding the pigs back at nightfall.

○

As it was high summer the evening Gathering was held outside in the middle of the circle of huts. First the Fire-Maker, a tall woman with a brown naked body and long black hair, built up the fire in the stone circle with twisted dry roots and broken branches, and when it was done and she had stepped back from the task, the Caller, a smaller woman, also wholly naked, cried out through her cupped hands, "Gather, Gather, Gather," making the call first to where the sun had set and then to the north and to the east and the south.

The tribe came together quickly, some emerging from the stone huts, some returning from work in the small quarry cut into the edge of the hill, and some coming along the track from the wooded country below. The women were all naked, as were the children. The older men were naked also, but those who came from the direction of the woodland, and some others, wore skins to protect their loins.

The first man to arrive was white-bearded, bent, the colour of ripe acorns, and he leaned upon a staff. He sat on one of the several rocks arranged about the fire. The Caller, her task performed, sat upon another, as did the third arrival, a woman of commanding presence whose long hair had been plaited into three coarse ropes, the central one of which hung down her back, the other two coming over her shoulders and lying each side of her breasts.

In a short time all were assembled. There were thirty or forty of them including children. Some women were nursing babies. One or two of them were pregnant. The woman with the three plaits opened the proceedings by saying "I Choose the beginning," after which the Caller said matter-of-factly, "She is with us, within us, around us, and we are together in Her."

She then looked at the white-bearded man who leaned forward and said, "I am very long-minded, and so I am the Talker though only a not-woman. I have in my long mind so many happenings and so many thinkings. There have been many thinkings. Many years ago there was a thinking that the year should be of ten-and-two moons, not ten only, for then the great cold and the great heat would happen always at the one place. But it was said that it is in Her nature to be the Maker of Change, and that She made the year to change, and, moreover that we have only ten to the hands and ten to the feet and if it was meant for us to think in ten-and-two's She would have brought birth to hands with ten-and-two and feet with ten-and-two, so that was all put aside. There was one who said he was ever-minded and who said he had seen that the year was ten-and-three moons but we laughed at him. There are many who say they are ever-minded and who are not so. I tell you this because being long-minded I have many words of the ever-minded in me and I know they were not always true words."

○

The young girl at the edge of the circle looked down at her crossed legs. They were thin, like twigs. She moved them a little and wriggled her toes. "I am Twig-Thin Stiff-Walker" she told herself. "But in a moon that is to come I will be Bird-Sender Life-Breather or Fire-Handed Far-Seer". She smiled to herself and wiggled her big right toe. It was a round brown root, she decided. It was of the earth. The Talker's voice was droning on. She looked at him seated across the fire from her. "A little tree," she said. "A little tree with two leaves on it," for he was gesturing with his hands.

As she stared, not listening to the words, she felt a familiar warmth in her head, and a tingling. She let it grow. "I am ever-minded," she told herself in a whisper, and she caught her breath just for a moment, and then breathed deeply, steadily, as she had learned, and the little tree that was the Talker grew tall, and the two leaves on the two bare branches were not leaves but the stone points of spears and they glittered in the firelight, and the words were not words but the sound of wood crackling in the fire. There was no light in the sky now. There was only the stain of firelight on the tall shape, and the girl shuddered, and the warmth drained away from her head. It was over. She looked round the circle. No one had seen her go into near-sleep. No one was looking. She herself looked round the circle of the Kindred and then at the stone huts behind them. Was there another thinking to come to her?

The roughly shaped stones of the round huts were dark. The light of the fire did not reach them. The big food hut and the kindling hut beside it looked darker than the rest. She began to breathe deeply once

11

more, looking at the openings into the huts. They were mouths. They were open mouths. From one of the mouths a thing was coming. It was a thing with hair on it. It was black. It had eyes. She stared, but it had gone and the near-sleep was gone also. She pushed her hands against the earth on either side of her and pressed her feet into the ground.

"That was a two-seeing," she told herself. "I must have a thinking in this dark."

And she turned her face again towards the Talker.

○

The Kindred were still in talk. The words were dry leaves rustling and twigs crackling. Three-Birth Reed-Twister was saying in her gentle voice "I have it from Her, for I am often ever-minded nowadays, that the year should be of nine moons for that is Her number, and indeed from the first food-spillings at morning to the birth-bringing is often nine moons. I am one who knows.

"Should we then cut off one finger, one toe?" The Talker frowned.

"I am suddenly ever-minded," said Black-Haired Deer-Walker, "and I count the holes in woman and there are ten holes. The two for listening, the two for seeing, the two of the nose, the one for speaking and eating, the one for voiding the yellow-water, the one for voiding body-earth, and the one for pleasure with not-woman."

"You have forgotten," said She-Who-Has-Born-Many, "the two breast holes that make woman the first-feeder, and that brings the number to ten-and-two."

There was a silence. "I am short-minded," said Big-Mouthed Child Gatherer, "But I have a thinking that it is because woman has ten-and-two holes and not-woman only nine that Chooser is always a woman in all things from pleasure-choosing to Callings, no matter what a not-woman may say, be he long-minded and Talker or not." She pursed her lips with mockery and made a false love-mouth at the Talker.

The Talker rallied. "It is," he said, "the task of the Talker to bring things to the circle. It is the task of the Chooser to listen and choose."

"I have listened," said the Chooser, crossing her arms upon her full brown breasts, "and though I am, as is the way, the Chooser only until the great cold finds ending and the first flowers shine, I am the Chooser. Here is only talk and thinkings. There is nothing to choose. I do not speak about these things. Let the Talker continue."

○

Gifting-Herder With Black Eyes stirred uneasily. The talk was wind shaking leaves. It was not a big wind. He thought about the stone head, and about Her. The stone was round. It was moon. It was sun. It was a full belly. It was the way the people sat around the fire making the shape of the moon. But the eyes were not moon eyes. He had seen eyes in the moon. They were eyes of mist. The stone eyes were hard. His thinking touched them, and his fingers moved back quickly. There was a hurt in them. Not a big hurt but a hurt like eye-water. A deep hurt.

Talker was still talking. There was no light in the sky now. There was only the light of the fire, but the knife moon would soon come up from over the hill. The fire crackled and Fire-Maker threw on another log. For a moment the firelight shook and sent new shapes. On Talker's belly, as he sat upright, straight-backed, it sent a shape like the stone head of a tree-breaker from the hands of the Maker. It was not round like a belly. It had four sides like the four sides of a gifting, but it was red, not gifting colour. It was there for three breaths and then it was gone. The lad shook his head. What was it he had seen? Was it from the ever-mind? He had no thinking. He put it aside carefully as he had put aside the black feather he had found by the stone face. It was a feather to stroke with and to see shine in. He had put it aside under the bracken strewn bedskins in the hut he shared with two other lads. He suddenly wanted to touch it. But Talker was still talking.

○

"It has been said," the Talker went on, "that She is the Maker of Change, and I have a thinking of a change to make. Till this very moon we all have long-callings and our short-callings are only used when there is hurry or deep quiet or other things of that kind. Yet it has come to me that all that is should have short-callings, so that even the short-minded can call in the right way and be called in the right way. Two darks ago I became ever-minded and heard the short-callings of many. They were given by Her, the All-Giver, the Change Maker, the Owner of all callings. Just as we ourselves have a Chooser to choose the calling and a Caller to say the calling, to say the changes in callings here every full round of the moon, so She was Chooser and Caller. It was not the

13

full round of the moon two darks ago, as you know. It was the new knife moon, but in my ever-mind I saw Her holding the full round of the moon in Her hand. The giftings she called Paeg, and Thick-Haired Howling Runner and Lurker she called Wolf, and Eye-Swallower Hoarse-Caller she called Kraw and to each one of us she gave a new calling. To Gifting-Herder With Black Eyes She gave Gron; to Black-Haired Deer-Walker She gave Fleay; to Thick-Armed Spear-Hurler She gave Harn; to Coldflowing Fish-Bearer She gave River; to Long-Eared Fur-Leaper she gave Hare; to Pink-Linked Wriggle-Finger She gave Wirm; to Three-Birth Reed-Twister She gave Bode; and so it was with all that are here and some that are not, though she did not give to some that already have short-callings such as yellow-water, mouth, nose, body-earth, finger, toe, and those others we all know. And She made it happen in me that all things had a short-calling and only some also a long-calling and that long-callings should be used only at Gatherings in the full round of the moon. That was the happening and the thinking."

There was a silence. "Though only a not-woman," said the Protector, "and only chosen Protector because I am strong and my long-calling is Thick-Armed Spear-Hurler, and not for my thinkings, I have a thinking that Harn is quicker to call and better to hold in the mind, and I will be Harn if the Caller makes it so."

"My long-calling pleases me," said the Maker, "for each time I am called it is put into my mind what I am and must be and do. I am Knife-Fingered Thong-Wristed Stone-Fisted Birth-Bringer and the only not-woman to be called birth-bringer, though those that help me are called birth-helpers. What is my short-calling to be?"

The Talker smiled. "It is a good short-calling," he said, "It is simply Maker."

The Maker groaned. "But some time I will no longer be Knife-Fingered Thong-Wristed Stone-Fisted Birth-Bringer," he said, "but maybe White-Headed, Stiff-Wristed, Mist-Eyed Hearthsweeper, not even Fire-Maker for that must be a woman. Then shall I still be called Maker?"

The Talker bit his lip. "This is a twisted path to climb," he said, "and one with many earth-twig foot-catchers. I have no thinking."

"The women will gather," said the Chooser, "and the women will do a thinking and the ever-minded will tell what they see and we will all be ever-minded together for a time, but it is my thinking that short-calling is good as long as long-calling is kept for the circle at the full round of the moon."

"That is the way," said the Talker gravely, "and it would be good if all the women became ever-minded together and therefore Her mind and could give Her a short-calling, and yet it is in me that She should have three short-callings for the beginning time, the time of ripeness, and the time of cold for these are Her three great changes."

"The women will meet," said the Chooser. "Is the talk over?"

"It is over," said the Talker, his face ruddy in the light of the fire, his white beard shining. "It is over for this dark."

"It is well," said the Chooser, and the Caller said, "In Her womb we lie this dark, and in our bodies She keeps Her presence."

One of the men went away and came back with meat, and both women and men put the meat to the fire on long pointed sticks. Two women brought baskets made of reeds in which were cakes of pressed berries wrapped in leaves, and other food. Three young women fetched and passed around drinking vessels made of baked clay. Each person at the first swallow of the liquid said perfunctorily, "In Her this dark."

In a little while, after some general conversation, the group broke up, each going his or her way, some in couples and some not, except for one man who remained by the fire, a spear at his side. A two day old moon drifted out of the cloud. In the distance a wolf howled.

○

Wide-Eyed Earth-Fast Breath-Sounder, the Caller, climbed to the top of the hill overlooking the dwelling place. Her brow was furrowed. Yet again she had been with the Talker since the day was made, and now it was the time of high heat, and she was weary. There were so many short-callings to know now, and everything would be changed. For many moons she had, sometimes in near-sleep and with the ever-mind, and sometimes simply in thinkings, brought the long-callings to birth, altering many each moon, for the Chooser would always listen to her and bow to her, even though it was supposed to be the Chooser who brought the new or altered callings to birth. Now it was different. Three-Birth Reed-Twister, whose earlier long-callings were Deer-Eyed Leg-Clutcher, Round-Breasted Loin-Surger, Big-Breasted Birth-Maker and many more, had now the short-calling Bode, and those she had brought to birth were short-called Bodwith, Bodwoth, and Bodweerth.

Three, and none met breath-ending at birth-bringing like so many. But there was no sound, no joy in it. Only at the full round of the moon would Bodwith be long-called Bright-Eyed Bird-Singer, and Bodweerth Flower-Mouthed Thread-Twister. She would remember all somehow, for she was the Caller, but who else would remember? And she had made a new long-calling for Black-Haired Deer-Walker too; it was to be Red-Lipped Loin-Shudderer. She wondered if the hint would be taken. More and more she preferred bed-sharing to choosing. She felt that it brought her closer to the Her all about and the Her within and to Her voice that she must somehow be, in the ever-mind or through near-sleep.

She sat on a rock at the top of the hill and recited the new short-callings that the Chooser was sure to say yes to, and to which nobody, save maybe Red-Lipped Loin-Shudderer, would say no. Start with that one. Fleay, Bode (the women first of course) Ranna, Liff, Tand, Brig, Meer, Sanna, Swess, Frig...

The sun was at his highest heat. Her eyelids were heavy. There was yet some time until the full round of the moon. She lay back on the hilltop, her brown nakedness shiny with sweat, and closed her eyes. Wirra, she murmured, Veld, Panka... and slept.

○

It was the full round of the moon and Black-Haired Deer-Walker stirred uneasily on her bracken bed. She had not chosen a not-woman for the night and her aloneness became suddenly a part of her.

"Now I am Black-Haired Lone-Sleeper," she told herself, "and not Deer-Walker at all."

She thought about the short-callings that had been brought to birth at the Gathering, and about the long-callings that were still inside her.

"If I was Deer-Walker before day was taken, and now in the dark I am Lone-Sleeper, then what is this that I am?" she asked herself. "I am Fleay?" she queried, making the calling slowly and carefully, feeling it first between her teeth and the lip, then on the flicking tongue tip, then as a little wind in the cheek and a sigh from the open mouth. "Fleay," she repeated. "I could be Fleay for all the moons and all the years, but I cannot be Black-Haired Deer-Walker for those times. Some moon I will grow heavy from birth-bringing and I will be Black-Haired Bear-Walker, for I will walk heavily like a bear. And then when I am first feeding I will be Black-Haired Baby-Suckler, and then after many many moons no longer black-haired at all. Then one will come who has been away and he will say 'Where is Black-Haired Deer-Walker?' and there will be no one of that calling, or if there is such a one it will not be me. But if I am Fleay then I am Fleay and I am not called by what I look like and by what I do but by what I am.

"I am," she told herself, almost biting her full red lower lip on the first sound, "Fleay.

"Fleay, Fleay," she repeated, and then, suddenly frightened, "Is it wrong to have one short-calling and not many changing long-callings?" she asked Her within. "Is it to make myself different from the moons which change, and the grasses and the trees and Cold-Flowing Fish-Bearer who is kind to my skin in the great heat and is harder than my bone in the great cold? Is it to become an outer-thing as Thick-Necked Woman-Thruster became an outer-thing when he pleasure-chose like a woman, where he was not chosen, and was beaten with sticks and sent away and told that if he ever came back to the Kindred, it would be that he was a gifting and good for filling bellies?"

She licked her lips and wondered if a not-woman would taste like a gifting, or perhaps like a deer or a wolf or a bear, though she had never eaten of bear and only once of wolf.

"He might," she thought, "be like Pink-Linked Wriggle-Finger that the Talker short-called Wirm, or at least one part of him might taste like that."

She giggled. She felt like pleasure-choosing but it was long past the proper choosing time. She rubbed her fur-hole gently and then stopped. She could wait until daymaking and then she would choose a good not-woman, perhaps Big-Toothed Wolf-Catcher, for Soft-Handed Fish-Taker had told her he pleasured well. She thought about Soft-Handed Fish-Taker and that only a moon ago she had been long-called Soft-Handed Woman-Rubber because after one Gathering at the full round of the moon she had not chosen but had bed-shared with another woman. Ten moons ago the Talker had been a long-minded woman, and *that* Talker had said that women should choose each other in the five moons after birth-bringing and at other times too if they wished, and that long-minded women who had born many should choose other women to bed-share. Such thinkings wrinkled her brow and she felt sleep covering first her legs, then her belly and her arms, and, ever so slowly, her throat, her mouth, her cheeks, her eyelids and, at the last, her place of thinking. "Fleay," she said to herself and not quite to the Her inside her, "Fleay," and she slept.

○

The lad stood by the stone face in the wall of the day's beginning and spoke to it. He said, "You know I am only a not-woman and because I have lived only ten times ten moons and four times ten moons more I am still very short-minded, but sometimes I have the near-sleep and then for the time of five breaths I am ever-minded and I see what the Talker tells me only women can see and only long-minded women at that. Is it You who make this in me?"

A briar wisped across the stone face. A crow lit on the wall and cocked its head to one side, beak open, as if it were listening and about to speak. The boy looked at the crow.

"Eye-Swallower, Hoarse-Caller," he said thoughtfully, "you are being changed to me by the old Talker who says that short-calling is good, that you are short-called Kraw, that I am short-called Gron instead of Gifting-Herder with Black Eyes. How can this be right? Some moon I may be 'Stone-Sharpener with Small Beard' not Gifting-Herder. Will I then still be Gron? Some moon you will be Black Feather and Bone Pile. Will you then be Kraw? The old Talker is a not-woman also; can a not-woman make callings when it is woman that is the birthmaker, and the first-feeder, and the pleasure-chooser? Are not-women to begin choosing women to their beds now, and are they going to give first food, from their ears maybe, or their thumbs?"

The crow stood on one leg. Black plumage glistened in the shadowcasting light. The stone face blew the briar aside through unmoving smiling lips.

"If I am Gron," said the boy to the stone face, "then I am not You as I know I am when I am ever-minded. Then, I am You and You are me, and I am earth and water and bush and berry and even the giftings with their grunts and twisty tails; I am part of them and they of me because I can be that which grunts and snuffles and that which lies still under trees, and that which flows shuddering over stones, and that which runs and that which cries and that which sleeps, but can Gron be these things?"

He scratched his nose.

"Sometimes," he said, "Black-Haired Deer-Walker is also Loin-Stirrer and chooses one not-woman and then another one. But sometimes, too, she is Water-Bringer, Stone-Washer, Berry-Gatherer. How then can she be short-called Fleay as the Talker says? And You who are all the callings and the longest calling of all and are always ever-minded alike, and old and young, and everything that happens, are we to short-call You too? The old Talker is saying You must have three short-callings. He says one could be Bo for that is a sudden birth-breath and You are all birth and breath. He says Raya for that is a tongue moving like a branch in a big wind. He says Ahhh for that is the sound of breath-ending and the breath that is carried back into Your womb. If when I call You Bo or Raya or Ahhh I think 'She who is all and everything in us and about us and of us and the Birth-Bringer of all', will that be right? I think as the moons pass and I become long-minded I may forget, and if I forget so will others forget and You will be soon no more than an old stone in a wall and we will listen to the Talker and not talk to You who give us talk in our own voices, each to each, and yet in Your voice too."

He stopped. Tears shone in his dark eyes. The crow jumped to one side and cried a harsh derisive squawk. The boy turned his back on the wall and looked up the hillside at the rooting pigs. It was evening and time to bring them into their place for the night away from the danger of wolves.

"Giftings," he said, "fat, lovely giftings, will you be happy to be short-called Paeg and for it to be forgotten that you give yourselves to us for meat, and skins, and bladders to make us water-movers, and sharp bones to make us skin-thinners, and so much more? Paeg is a bad calling for you," he said, "There is no giving in it".

TWO

Some distance from the group of stone huts and above them, cut into the hillside, was a cave, and seated outside it a woman whose black hair was streaked with grey. She was quite still, cross-legged, and staring out over the village with unfocussed eyes. She had been sitting there ever since dawn and it was now well past noon. The woman short-called Fleay since the Gathering at the full round of the moon was seated a little distance away and watching her with an expression of impatience. It was very irritating of Fire-Handed Breath-Changer to stay so long in near-sleep she told herself. But then that woman was often irritating. She did not pleasure-choose like the other women, and she did not even bed-share. Nor did she hunt or fish or gather as other women and not-women did. She went away often, too, and did not come to all of the gatherings. Sometimes she even missed the great gathering at the full round of the moon. Fleay gritted her teeth. Perhaps the hurting would go away without help. Perhaps if she said firmly "Hurting be gone," it would go. She said aloud, "Hurting be gone!"

It did not go. She wished that there was not a strong thinking that no one should wake another from near-sleep, but it was a very strong thinking indeed and she dared not go against it. Maybe if she went up the hill behind the cave and her foot made a stone roll down near Fire-

Handed Breath-Changer it would not be wrong. She rubbed her belly. The hurting was getting bigger and bigger. She could not help herself. She uttered a great wail of pain and fury.

The cross-legged woman stirred and said, as if she had been waiting for that very sound, "Come."

Fleay went, her hands on her belly, hunched a little with the pain, and the older woman stood up.

"I have a hurting," said Fleay. The woman nodded. She held out her right hand, fingers splayed, so that it did not quite touch the girl's belly, and closed her eyes. Her hand seemed to mould itself in the air to the shape of the belly.

After a few breaths she said, "There is a wrongness I cannot reach. There are reeds between my fingers and the fish."

Fleay felt herself blushing. "It is a thinking," she said, "I had a bad thinking. It was a very bad thinking."

"What was it?" asked the woman.

Fleay hesitated. "I had a thinking," she said, "that I should wake you from near-sleep."

"That is not it," said the woman.

Fleay wriggled.

"I had a thinking to pleasure-choose the big gifting," she almost whispered, "and as I was lone-sleeping I rubbed my fur-hole and had a pleasuring and it was the big gifting in my fur-hole."

The woman smiled. "It is not that thinking that stops my fingers," she said. "It is this new thinking that it was bad. Now I take that thinking that it was bad away from you," and she made a sign in the air with her hands. "Now," she said, "I can reach the fish," and the warmth spread down her arms from her shoulders, and, feeling the familiar hot tingle in her fingers and in her palms, she pressed her hand against the air a finger's breadth away from the girl's belly.

"It is hot," said Fleay, and then, "It is going."

"It has gone," said the older woman smiling.

"That is right," said Fleay. She looked down at her belly and rubbed it affectionately. "It comes to me that I will make body-earth now," she said and swung away down the hill, remembering just in time to call back over her shoulder, "In Her, Through Her."

"In Her, Through Her" responded the older woman, and laughed. Many many moons ago she had been like that girl herself; self-

22

confident, greedy for life, energetic, and, she supposed, a little comical. That was before she was Taken. She remembered the Taking.

It was when she was gathering berries in the woodland, a young girl only three moons after her first blood-flow. She came upon a pool hidden within bushes and as she looked down into it and saw her Other looking up at her—slim, naked, great-eyed—the Other became a mist and disappeared for the space of three breaths; and then, as she saw it again, a great heat filled her body, tingling her fingers, her face and her breasts; a sweat came up and she stood there in a burning, astonished but not as frightened as she told herself that she should be. It was as if a great cloak, a skin of heat, enveloped her. She spread her arms wide and it was as if all the leaves and the branches and the berries, even the earth under her and the water before her flowed into her through her stretched fingers. She looked up and the birds flying overhead seemed to enter her. Suddenly weak, she sat down cross-legged beside the pool and closed her eyes and fell into a near-sleep so deep that her body no longer felt. In that near-sleep she moved like water over all the land, as if she were a great flood; she flowed into the dwelling place and first it was Stone-Eyed Thong-Maker over whom she flowed, and he turned his face to her and his eyes were her eyes; then it was Bent-Legged Berry-Moulder, and she turned her head likewise and the eyes were her own eyes once again, and so on through the whole village; seeking out every one of the Kindred wherever they were, she flowed over them until at the last, when all had entered her she was no more a flood of water but a great fire, then suddenly a great cold, and the near-sleep left her, and she found herself no longer in the woodland by the pool but seated outside her own stone hut, shivering, although the day was hot, and some of the Kindred were standing round her.

"You have been walking in your near-sleep," said one of them gently.

Another said, "Look at her eyes and how she shivers. She has been Taken."

After that she lived with Great-Eyed All-Helper, who told her all the strong thinkings, and all the hidden thinkings, and taught her the big and small happenings, and the big talking and the small talking, and that was how it had all begun.

And now, she told herself, there was a changing. There had been many changings since she made the Wander those many many moons ago and returned to hear herself called Fire-Handed Breath-Changer at the gathering. There was the changing that came when not-women were given speech at the gatherings for the first time. There was the changing when the new strong thinking came that a not-woman could be Talker. And now there was the changing of long-callings to short-callings, not only for those that had always had short-callings but for all things. This changing did not disturb her. She had already seen, in near-sleep, the way that it would go. Already, even before the gathering when the short-callings were made birth by the Caller, the Kindred were playing with the thinking as children play with pebbles.

She thought of her own short-calling like a pebble and rolled it in her hands. "Manka," she said aloud, and again she laughed. Whatever the short-callings, the living was in Her and the living was Her and Manka would be Fire-Handed Breath-Changer still, and also River-Shining Sleep-Bringer, Dark-Eyed Belly-Sweller, so many long-callings none of which could ever go away, not even when she would be long-called White-Haired Bent-Backed Tooth-Dropper.

She laughed again at this seeing of herself. "Manka," she said again, and then suddenly stiffened. There was a happening. She felt it inside her head. She put her fingers to her head and the fingers found the face of Twig-Thin Stiff-Walker, who had been Taken only ten moons ago, and to whom she was telling all the thinkings, happenings, and talkings so that when her own breath-ending came the Kindred would not be left helpless. Twig-Thin Stiff-Walker, now short-called Plara, was, she felt, breaking the reeds between herself and another, between herself and, she suddenly knew, a not-woman, and those reeds could never be broken. She put her finger to her throat and sent a bird-thinking, quickly. "Plara" was the bird she sent, already using the short-calling.

The bird did not return. She sighed with satisfaction. Plara would come to her. She put her finger to her head and looked for the face of the not-woman but saw only a gifting. It grunted and blinked its pink eyes. She would know soon enough. She waited.

Plara, alone, was gathering herbs in the near deep of the forest. To the far deep she would not go. That was for spear carriers and deer bringers. Through the trees she could hear other women and near-women talking and laughing. They were berry-picking. They were not Taken; they were not of the ever-mind.

"The Taken walk alone," she told herself.

24

It was a thinking of Manka, a deep thinking. She looked at the thinking and a not-woman stood beside it, a not-woman with black hair and black eyes.

"Gron," she said to herself, "Gron." And she found she was stretching out her hands towards him, and, quite suddenly, she felt a loin-stirring. She dropped her hands. There was a strong thinking against this. She was Taken. She must walk alone, or become an outer-thing and be driven far from the huts of the Kindred into the deep forest never to come back. She sent the not-woman that was Gron away. She put a thick mat of reeds between him and her, and as she did so there was a speaking in her head. The speaking was of Manka and it was calling her to the Cavern. She hesitated. She would not go yet; there were herbs to gather. She knelt down. Here were bruise-leaves and here nose-flowers. At the edge of the small clearing there would be soft moss. She told her hands to gather and her eyes to see only the herbs, and went on gathering.

○

Talker sat alone under a berry bush. He was in a rage, for he had twisted his leg and it was hurting, and yet he did not want to go to Manka. She would tell him there were reeds between her hands and the fish; she would say it was a thick mat of reeds, and she would perhaps send a hand into him and pull out his thinking. He could not do that. He had in his mind all the strong thinkings but she alone had the hidden ones, and so much more. Being a not-woman he could never have all the thinkings and happenings, be he ever so long-minded.

But at least he had done some things.

He had made it a strong thinking that not-women could have speech at the gatherings, and that had been moons ago. And now he had, himself, brought the short-callings to birth. If only he could make a strong thinking that not-women could pleasure-choose. Not every day, but every knife moon perhaps. Or perhaps only the not-women who were Helpers, such as Harn, the Protector, Maker, and, of course, Talker. He had not been chosen for many moons. He would choose Fleay the first knife moon, and Farla the moon following. He wanted to choose Manka but Manka did not choose ever. Little Plara would not choose either. The Taken could not pleasure-choose or even bed-share.

His ankle was hurting badly. He gritted his teeth and stood up cautiously. It was a bad hurting. He sat down again. If Manka were made an outer-thing and sent away, then little Plara would be easy. She would soon know all the thinkings, happenings, and talkings. In ten more moons maybe he could tell the Kindred that Manka had pleasure-chosen, that he had seen it, and he could say that Harn had seen it, and then she would be an outer-thing and sent away.

He grinned to himself. If she became an outer-thing he could follow her into the woodland a little way and he could choose her; Harn could be a helper for he was strong, and there was no strong thinking about not-women choosing an outer-thing. There was no thinking about that at all. Perhaps he should make a strong thinking that outer-things can be . . .

He made a casual movement and yelped with pain. It would have to be Manka. He could not go to her. She must come to him. He tried a bird-thinking but it did not fly. Soon it would be near-dark and Caller would start the Gathering. Then they would look for him. There could not be a Gathering without the Talker. Harn would look for him.

He was exhausted. He tried another bird-thinking. The bird did not even shape itself.

○

Plara laid the bag of herbs she had gathered aside upon the bole of a dark twisting tree and looked down into the pool. It was brown, the colour of bear, deep as near-sleep, and still as a breath-taken bird. It was, her tingling fingers and the sudden heat of her body told her, a Watching Pool. She put her legs apart and planted her feet as firm as roots upon the damp earth. She sent her arms out from her body and spread her fingers and looked into the pool and her Other looked up at her.

As she stared at her Other, the thin bony face, the small breasts, the twig-thin arms and legs, the black-tufted fur-hole, moving herself through ever-mind into near-sleep, the Other blurred and became Fire-Breath, grey then silver-white, then parted and she saw Gron. He was seated upon a stone. The giftings were rooting and snuffling about him. As she watched he turned his face towards her and his eyes were grey pebbles with no seeing in them and his mouth moved and he picked up a twig from between his feet, holding one end in one hand and one in the other. There was sweat upon his forehead, and he broke the stick, whereupon there was a great rippling before her and the pool was a pool again, but no longer still, as if some great stone had fallen into it, and she woke from near-sleep with a start; her body was cold and she was trembling.

She sat down on the bole beside her gatherings. "That was a deep-seeing," she told herself, "and I have no clear thinking. But it comes to me that Gron was breaking a twig that must not be broken."

She stopped shivering and went back to the pool and looked again. Her Other stared at her. The pool was still as Cold-Flowing Fish-Bearer in the great cold. Her Other did not change.

She said slowly, "It comes to me that this is a happening that brings hurtings. It comes to me that I have a loin-stirring for Gron and there is a strong thinking against that, for I have been Taken. It comes to me that I have not been all the way Taken or I would not have this loin-stirring. I am half the twig and not all of it.

"Gron" she mused, "is a not-woman and cannot be Taken, but I have a thinking that if he were a woman he would be Taken. He is half the twig. We are two half-twigs, Plara and Gron. He broke a twig to send a bird-thinking to me?" she asked herself. "No. It was not to me that he sent the bird-thinking."

She sighed. She picked up her bundle of gatherings and began to walk back through the forest to the dwelling place. A crow squawked onto a branch ahead of her and cocked its head.

"Kraw," she said aloud, still feeling the short-calling uncomfortable though it had been two moons since the Gathering when short-callings had been brought to birth. "You who are Her as all things are Her and In Her and Through Her, help me to a clear thinking."

She planted her feet apart again and sent two deep roots into the earth, feeling the deep-reaching flow up into her, and she closed her eyes, setting a binding upon the bird as she had been taught to do. Then she opened her eyes and the crow perched still upon the bough and the thinking came to her clear as the voice of the Caller on a still clear night in the time of ripeness.

Twigs are breaking, came the voice into her, *and the breakings will make fire and the fire will be a new fire and the old fire will be grey ash on the wind.*

She felt the deep-reaching flow back into the earth and the crow flapped one black wing, then the other, and then both together and

27

lurched upwards through the trees and was gone. Plara frowned. "I have been all the way Taken," she told herself, "for I have near-sleep and can set a binding upon Kraw and Paeg and the deep fish and upon tree, and soon I will set a binding upon the Kindred when it comes to me that it must be done. I am all the way Taken, but still I have loin-stirrings. Is the strong thinking against loin-stirrings in the Taken a twig that will be broken? Is it the twig that Gron was breaking?"

She felt a little jump in her breast and caught her breath. "The bird-thinking was not for me," she added to herself, "but I have a clear thinking that it was a deep thinking he broke. And he who breaks a deep thinking must have a hurting, and could become an outer-thing." She shuddered. "Manka," she said, "Manka will give me a hidden thinking." She was now at the edge of the forest and, looking up, she saw the stone walls of the gifting place on the hill dark against the sky.

○

Gron herded the last gifting into the stone enclosure and blocked the entrance to it. He stood once again before the stone face, and pulled the briars and bracken away so that he could see it more clearly.

"It is my thinking," he said "that Plara... " He paused. "Short-callings are not for this," he said. "This is deep thinking."

He stared into the stone eyes. There was a speck of lichen at one eye corner. He picked it off gently.

"It is my thinking," he said, "that Twig-Thin Stiff-Walker is ready to pleasure-choose and that Gifting-Herder With Black Eyes is ready to be chosen, but Twig-Thin Stiff-Walker must not pleasure-choose for there is a strong thinking against that, and Gifting-Herder With Black Eyes will not be chosen by her." He scratched his head. "You are me and I am You," he said, "and in my ever-mind there is a dark thinking that though I am a not-woman I have so much near-sleep that I could be Taken, as Twig-Thin Stiff-Walker was Taken. How strong are the strong thinkings?" he asked, "Are there near-sleep happenings that can break them?"

He sat cross-legged in front of the stone face and gazed up at the big blind eyes. "It comes into me," he said, "that it is the Talker who has brought some strong thinkings to birth and he is a not-woman; but be-cause he is long-minded his strong thinkings are a loud hearing to the Chooser and to the Caller and to all women and not-women. But it is

Fire-Handed Breath-Changer only who has in her mind the hidden thinkings and the big talkings and many secret things, and Twig-Thin Stiff-Walker is to have these things in her mind also; and though the Caller brings callings to birth and tells the strong thinkings and the story at the full round of the moon, she does not have the hidden things in her mind; and though the Chooser chooses the thinkings the Caller brings to birth she does not have the hidden things in her mind. And the Talker is only long-minded and knows no hidden things but only what all women and all not-women see and touch and hear and do and the happenings of many moons. This the Caller does not hold in her mind, for her mind is filled only with the story and the callings. I have a dark thinking that the Chooser and the Caller and the Talker all in one body together have not the way into Your Womb and the way out of Your Womb that Fire-Handed Breath-Changer walks in her near-sleep and that Twig-Thin Stiff-Walker will walk also."

He bit his lip and said slowly, "It is a way I would walk," and then he said "Oh," and he felt a great heat flowing into him and a great dark also, and he sat there still as the stone head before him. It was now twilight and the voice of the Caller came to him, "Gather, Gather, Gather," and it seemed to him that it was in his belly. He heard it again and it was in his chest. The third time it was inside his head and he opened his eyes and the cry of *Gather Gather Gather* was all about him like a flock of birds and he was awake and suddenly very cold, and dizzy. He bowed his head and said with a catch in his voice, "In You, Through You." Then the cold went away and he stood up and walked down the hill to the Gathering.

○

The old woman had not gone to the Gathering. She lay very still upon her bed of bracken in the cool darkness of the stone hut, her breathing shallow, the sharply defined rib cage moving up and down as quickly as that of a spent and wounded wolf. Manka sat cross-legged beside her, watching.

The old woman stirred in her sleep and opened her eyes. "My deep thinking tells me," she whispered, "that I am for the giftings."

Manka nodded. "You are deep-sleeping into Her Womb," she said, "and there will be another breath-finding for you when She gives you that happening."

The woman sighed. "I had a thinking many moons ago that I would be the Talker," she said, "for I was long-minded and Talker is not more long-minded than I, but at that full round of the moon I had a hurting and the Chooser. . . . " her voice trailed away like a vine withered upon a wall, dried and dwindling.

"In Her, Through Her, all happenings," said Manka.

The old woman coughed feebly. "When my body is put before the giftings," she said, "will the Caller bring to breath all my long-callings as was the strong thinking when I was short-minded, or will it be only my short-calling that walks back into Her womb?"

Manka said very softly, spreading her hands out over the old woman's body, "I speak to you now in your deep mind and mine, and set this binding upon you that we speak." The old woman said nothing but closed her eyes in submission. "White-Haired Twig-Armed Still-Sitter," she said, "Grey-Haired Round-Backed Thong-Maker, Dark-Eyed Strong-Armed Skin-Worker, Black-Haired Firm-Fingered Deer-Flayer, Great-Eyed Round-Bellied Birth-Bringer, Red-Lipped White-Toothed Loin-Stirrer, Quick-Legged Thin-Armed Berry-Gatherer, Sharp-Voiced Brown-Skinned Loud-Shouter, Fat-Toed Fat-Legged Earth-Crawler, Bright-Eyed Wet-Skinned Breast-Nuzzler, Wild-Haired Bear-Walker's Womb-Opener."

The old woman, eyes still closed, offered the words a small hesitant smile. Manka bent forward. "I speak to you," she said and, sinking into deep-sleep, saw before her, in the centre of a mist, the face of the old woman which shifted as she watched from age to youth to childhood and back again until it became all those faces and yet only one.

"You know this is your time of breath-ending," said Manka, "and it is the time of last speaking."

The woman's lips moved and said gently, "I know this. I am in all my happenings and I carry them up the path I am set upon."

"Are the happenings heavy?"

"Some are heavy and some are light."

"Give me the heavy happenings that I may bear them for you."

The woman's face altered, changed colour, became first pallid then grey, the lips blue, and the eyes were hurt. "Four times I pleasure-chose against the wanting of a not-woman, and it was a great hurting to him. I told myself that it was in the strong thinking that I could choose and so I chose, but I have a deep thinking that there was a hurting in Her womb."

"This I will carry."

"In the forest I heard my Other speak and would not listen, having a fear I might be Taken, and I ran from the forest and pleasure-chose two times in that day and I have a deep-thinking that Her eyes were weeping."

"This I will carry."

"On the moon that Talker was called and I was not called I had a thinking that Talker put the hurting in my belly and this thinking will not go from me; it has been a hurting in me for many moons and because it is a hurting in me it is a hurting in Her."

"This I will carry."

"I have more but I cannot speak them. My feet are on the path."

"I carry them all."

"In Her, Through Her, All Things, All Ways."

"In Her, Through Her, All Things, All Ways."

The woman's face changed, the colour became normal, the skin clearer, the mouth lost its blueness, the eyes grew bright. It was almost a face of a young woman and as it melted in the mist Manka saw beyond it and within it the figure of a sturdy woman walking a straight track up a hill. Sweat upon her brow, she took a deep breath, and, weight upon her shoulders, walked up that hill herself until she and the walking figure were one, until in front of her there was a cavern much like her own cavern. There she stopped and the weight fell from her shoulders and the other woman went ahead of her into the cave and Manka spoke aloud as she stood at the mouth of the cave, and said, "It is given and it is taken."

The cave faded away into mist which dissolved into pure darkness. Manka opened her eyes. The old woman lay still in death. Manka stood up. She was exhausted. She pushed the hair back from her brow and went out of the stone hut. She pulled the loose stone always set above the doorway free from its earth-bed and placed it on the threshold as a sign that breath had been taken and made her way slowly across the now empty Gathering space to the hut where the Caller was waiting.

○

THREE

Seated at the edge of the gathering, withdrawn from the company a little, behind the first circle of the Kindred, Gron only half listened to Talker. He was puzzling over the twig he had broken. It had come to him to break the twig but he did not know what twig he had broken.

"It was a deep thinking," he told himself, "and it was a happening in deep sleep and so it was In Her and Through Her."

He shuddered. The Talker's voice broke through his meditation. "Henda has found breath-ending, and for one dark and one day she has been in Her womb and She has not sent her back down the path to breath-beginning. There is a strong thinking," Talker said ponderously, "and it is that when breath has been taken and not given again, the body is put before the giftings at the next coming of light, and the giftings eat and the body is again Hers."

Gron nodded automatically in unison with the whole gathering.

"There is another strong thinking," said Talker, "and it is that, when the giftings have eaten, all that has not entered their bellies is thrown into the water and put before the fish and the fish eat and this part is again Hers. I have seen in my ever-mind that this is not good. When water is not fast-flowing but still and stiff a bad-breathing comes from the waters, and when the water is stiff as bone in the big cold it is a hard-breaking to place the body before the fish.

"Many moons ago in the time of heat the water was thin and did not cover the body parts given the fish and the bad-breathing was strong and sickness came. I have seen in my ever-mind and in near-sleep a new strong thinking—it is that the body should be put upon a big fire at the coming of dark; the big fire should be made upon the top of the big hill; and the fire-breath of it will be in Her nose-holes. She will take in the fire-breath and be strong in that breath and clear speaking in our deep-sleep and it will be a loud hearing. It has come to me that this place of burning should have stones about it, and that there should be long-minded ones watching through the dark; the watchers will go into deep-sleep and in that deep sleep thinkings will come to them and they will be clear thinkings and loud hearings with the new breath that She has been given."

He paused. Gron leaned forward. He had not spoken at a Gathering before and his throat was dry and scratchy as the grey tree-moss.

"The watchers will be women?" he asked.

Talker frowned. "Women or not-women," he said. "All are In Her, Through Her. It comes to me that the Watchers are long-minded, for the long-minded have had many near-sleeps and many deep thinkings and can tell a big fish from a little fish in the ripples. Short-minded ones can not do this."

There was a silence. Caller said, "There will be a big calling of all the long-callings?"

Talker answered, "It comes to me that the Watchers will make the calling through the dark."

Caller put her hands to her throat. "I have a hurting," she said. "There is a taking away in my neck. It is a hurting that is empty; a twig in the bundle is breaking."

Gron felt himself grow tense. He asked himself, "Is this the twig I broke? Did I break a twig in the neck of Caller?" He felt himself flushing.

Fleay lifted her head from contemplation of her splayed and wriggling toes. "Now that Henda has gone from us into the Womb," she said, "Talker is the longest-minded of the Kindred, and the other long-minded ones are Prand and Grek and they are not-women." She looked across the circle at Manka. "Not-women cannot be Taken" she said, "and it is the ones that have been Taken who have all the strong thinkings and the hidden thinkings and not the long-minded. It comes to me that Manka and little Plara are the Watchers about the big fire."

Talker wriggled uneasily on his stone. "Fleay is not the Chooser," he said, "and it comes to me that Plara is short-minded and new-Taken, and there are many darks when Manka must go to the Kindred and take away hurtings, and it could be a happening that there is a big hurting at the time of the body-fire and Manka is at the fire and cannot go."

The Gathering fell silent. Gron looked round at the Kindred. None were moving. All were looking at Manka, who was seated still as a stone. When she spoke she spoke softly.

"It is a big changing," she said, "and it comes to me that this is one twig in a bundle that is breaking and in one moon or two moons other twigs will break. She is Change and Change is In Her and Through Her. I am not the Chooser."

The heads turned to Chooser. Chooser said, "The giftings are fat and will only take small parts into their bellies. The water is thin and not fast-flowing, and a bad-breathing could come and many hurtings. Fire is In Her and Through Her. Talker's new strong thinking is deep and clear and makes a loud hearing. When this dark has been taken all will gather twigs and branches and take them up to the top of the hill and at the coming of the new dark it will be as Talker has seen in his deep-mind. I have chosen."

A sigh ran round the gathering. There was a pain in Gron's belly. It was not hunger. Manka stared blindly into the flickering flames.

○

The man called Skang lay easily in the sleeping place he had made for himself high in the big tree. He looked around him and, seeing that his bag of deer-hide was safely lodged and his bow and the seven long arrows were within reach, he composed himself to sleep. As so often before during his wanderings a picture came unbidden into his mind. He saw the circle of dark faces changing shape in the flicker of the fire-light, as if they were made of wet clay changing under the moulder's hand. He felt again the dryness in his throat and the trembling of his knees and heard the words, as he strained at the thongs of raw-hide that bound his wrists. It was the oldest of the men speaking, he with the horns of deer bound upon his head and a string of clattering deer hooves around his neck.

"The story has come to us," said the horned one, "and this is your story. When you came out of the womb you cried out a great cry and it was the cry of a wolf, but the woman that bore you did not heed the cry. When you were at the strength of bow-bending you looked on a man and the man fell and died, but it was not heeded. When you were at your first hunting you looked at a great deer and the deer leapt into the big water and was gone from us, but even this was not regarded. Now, however, your woman has born a child that is dead with a hump upon its back, and the story is told and understood."

Skang turned restlessly on his sleeping platform. The moon was bright and his mind would not empty itself of the circle of faces and of the words of the horned man that grew slower and softer until they were almost a whisper.

"The woman will be purified for many days and nights and when she can no longer speak your name she will be given to another man. If there were not a word against killing any member of the tribe you would be looking into the eyes of the Great Wolf that comes for all. We must obey the word, and so for three days you will run, and then you will no longer be of the tribe and we will send you to the Great Wolf if we come upon you."

The voice rose a little, the flames flickering hollows of black in the old face.

"Cut the bond."

Skang smiled grimly to himself at the memory of the knife slicing through the rawhide on his wrists, and at the sudden fierce joy with which he twisted that knife out of the man's hand and backing away from the fire cried "I am looking at *you*," and saw the faces suddenly startled, the mouths open, before he ran, at first stumbling a little from the cramp in his legs, into the forest. After that it was berries and water until he jumped upon a young deer from the tree in which he lay and cut its throat, and made himself a carrying bag, a thong for the bow he cut from a tree, and arrowheads from the splintered bones. But that was, he reflected, almost a moon ago. He looked up at the moon, and then glimpsed a light far away, a red glare. "Fire", he told himself, "a great fire". He stood up and stared. He felt suddenly more alone than ever before and his mind filled with pictures of men and women, oh very much with women, at a feast. The bough on which he stood pointed directly towards the fire. It was, he knew, directing him where to go.

○

It was almost dawn. The blue-grey light in the east behind the hill outlined the small hump of the dying fire and the three men standing around it, as Gron, creeping from the hut he shared with two other lads rubbed the sleep from his eyes, and took a gulp of the cool clean air. No one else was moving among the huts, and the Watcher beside the smaller fire was dozing with his back against a stone. Gron stretched himself lazily. He went down to the river which was running slug-gishly, its water dark except where the new light of day touched on an occasional ripple. He knelt on the edge of the bank and looked down into the water and his Other looked back at him, lean faced, black haired, the features shifting and reforming as he looked.

"In Her, Through Her," he said to himself sleepily and, on impulse, put his hand down to touch the Other, to make it break up and vanish into patches of darkness and then let it re-form. As his fingers met the water a shudder ran through his body, not the shudder of the cold that he had expected, but quite another sensation. It was as if the heat of a great fire had run up from the water into his arm and into his throat and face, and into his breathing. He closed his eyes, the better to feel this new goodness, for he knew it was good, and a mist filled his head. "I am in near-sleep" he told himself, and then, obscurely, "It is hap-pening," and as he told himself the words the mist in his head thick-ened and became the stone head of the gifting place, yet it was not wholly stone, for the eyes were alive and the lips moved, and he was suddenly on a high place, which was not a hill or a tree but another kind of height, looking down on the village, on the huts, the gifting place, the Gathering place with its firepit, and even the big fire on the big hill. As he watched the Kindred came out of their huts one by one, and as soon as he recognized any woman, not-woman or child, he or she knelt down, and in moments all were kneeling, even the Chooser and the Caller, and the Talker. He turned his eyes towards the cave and recognized Manka. Manka did not kneel. She stood up strong and proud and flung her arms out wide and he felt a great heat in him, a heat greater far than before, then a piercing cold, and with a sudden shock he was awake, lying flat on his face on the bank of the river. He was dizzy and faint. His right hand was in the water and it was clutching a black shining stone. Carefully he took the stone from the water and looked at it. It was the size of a child's fist, almost round and totally black. He knew he must hide it before the rest of the tribe came out of their huts. Knees shaking, he got to his feet and set out to the gifting place. He knelt down before Her and put the stone beside Her among the briar roots. Then and only then did he come fully to himself and, looking around him at a land that had changed in a deep unfathomable fashion, said half to himself and half to the stone face, "I have been Taken," and his eyes filled with tears.

○

Long before the time for the evening Gathering there were whisperings of the strong thinkings that had come to Talker during the burning of Henda. Prand and Grek, his companions of the night, told of the way in which Talker had suddenly become stiff as a big tree, standing so close to the fire that sparks flew upon his skin, and yet he did not move. They said he spoke from near-sleep and the words were as hard to break open as the big speckled stones beyond, and as rushing as the waters after the big cold. They said that the sparks had been like birds flying high, that they changed to birds and then to stars and that there were faces in the smoke and in the fire, faces of those who had returned to the Womb moons and moons ago. They said that when the Talker woke from near-sleep he almost fell and they had to hold him up, one on each side.

"The watchers must be three," said Prand pompously, "One to hear the strong thinkings and the hidden thinkings and two to stop the falling."

"There are three short-callings for Her," said Grek, "and three must be at the burning; but all this you will hear from Talker and it will be a loud hearing."

Gron heard little of all these things, for he stayed alone with the giftings, trying to understand what had happened to him. He wished to meet with nobody and even when little Plara came up the slopes to him he told her he had a hurting and must be alone. "It is a strong thinking that only women are Taken," he told himself, "and yet I am a not-woman.

"Was it a Taking?" he asked himself and he answered that it was a Taking. He felt inside his head and found another strong thinking, and it was that not-women who broke the strong thinkings were outer-things and would be beaten with sticks and sent away.

"But strong thinkings are a bundle of twigs and twigs have been broken," he told the biggest of the giftings, "and did not Manka have a thinking that many twigs will be broken and that a changing will come?"

He sat down on a rock and watched the giftings rooting and snuffling. He saw that a small gifting (not *Paeg*, he said to himself firmly, but *Gifting*) had a sore behind one ear. Almost without making a picture in his head, he reached out his hand towards the sore place and his head was filled with a picture of clean healed skin and a warmth ran down his arm from the shoulder and the small gifting stood very still. As the picture went away and the warmth lessened he knew he had taken a hurting away as only Manka of all the Kindred could take hurtings away. His body was trembling. He put a picture of a bird in his head and he sent the bird flying out. It flew quickly and strongly but he had no picture of where it was flying and no long-calling came to him for the bird to carry, and yet the bird was there. He called it back into his head and then he made it once more.

"Fire-Handed Breath-Changer," he commanded the bird, and "Come," he made the message, and sent the bird-thinking out. He stood up tall on the rock, watching and waiting, and it was not many breaths before he saw a figure coming up the slope towards him; it was Plara and, a little way behind her, Manka.

○

"It was a strong thinking and a hidden thinking and a big happening that came to me at the burning," said Talker, "I was bending my knees to sit upon a rock when my knees grew stiff as an unbroken bough and the fire-breath that had entered Her nose-holes came from Her mouth and into me and it was Her word and it was 'Talker is a big tree and a big tree does not bend,' so I stood there like a tree stands and it comes to me that I am a Talker here, and here I stand."

He lifted himself up from the rock with the help of his staff and stood upon the rock. There were gasps of surprise and shock from many of the gathering, for was there not also a strong thinking that at the Gathering none should stand but all should sit and only Caller, Chooser, Talker and Protector upon stones? Talker was thin and tall and stood high above all others so that the firelight shone only upon his legs and his belly and his face was in darkness. Chooser leaned forward. "You break a strong thinking, Talker," she said. "Are you then an outer-thing?"

Talker said slowly, steadily, "There is a changing, and the changing is that the strong thinkings are a bundle of twigs and when a twig dries it breaks and there must be another twig if the bundle is to be big for building a roof with Her clay and Her spittle."

Chooser frowned. "I do not choose," she said. "It is not a thing to choose at this dark," and she bit her lip.

"As I was a tree by that burning," said Talker, "Her breath was in my branches, and my roots were in Her womb, and my leaves were tens and tens and tens of tongues and they spoke with Her breath. It came to me then, in deep-sleep, that of the twigs of the tree a new bundle must be made, and there were three twigs in the bundle. The one-twig was the twig of the gathering, and I had a picture of the gathering in my head; all were seated but three, and the three that were standing trees were Chooser and Talker and Protector and the three trees were together, for three together are stronger than one when the great wind blows. But three trees that are tall have bareness near the ground so there must be bush and bracken, and in my picture between the fire and the trees there were three small strong bushes; they were Caller and Maker and Fire-Maker."

He paused. Fleay wriggled restlessly. "That is six twigs you have broken, Talker, and not one, and you have no tree that is the Healer, the Word-Sender, the holder of hidden thinkings and happenings. Is Manka not a big tree? She takes away our hurtings. She took away my belly hurting," she added as an unnecessary proof.

Talker drew a deep breath. "Those who are Taken," he said, "are in Her; they have their cavern away from the huts; they do no hunting and they do not pleasure-choose and they are not of the Kindred."

"Are they then outer-things?" said Vonga, a dark woman with a child at her breast.

"I have no thinking," said Talker, "They were not in the picture in my head."

He spoke more rapidly, hurrying his words over the difficulty. "The two-twig is the twig of blossoms. As I stood with Her breath my breath, and Her Womb my root, the three trees and the three bushes flowered, and it came to me that Chooser should have upon her a blossom and the blossom should be of the feathers of birds that fly in the air and walk upon the earth and move in the water for these birds choose the paths they go. And it came to me that Protector should have a blossom and it should be of the teeth of wolves and the claws of bears and round his neck, for Protector keeps these from us. Caller about her neck should have the skull and bones of Kraw, for Kraw is the loud caller in this place. Maker should have as blossom a covering for his head that is made of the skin of Paeg, for Paeg is made into tens and tens of things. Fire-Maker's blossom is of many dried leaves for they are the feeders of fire. Talker's blossom is a big staff bigger than a woman or a not-woman for Talker is a tree that speaks; there will be leaves bound on that staff in the hot times and berries upon that staff in the time of cold and he will wear a skin around his belly and down to his knees for that is the trunk of the tree. And no other one, woman or not-woman, shall have blossoms like these. That is the two-twig."

"What is the way of these blossoms?" asked Caller, "It comes to me that the blossoms are callings; it is not in my mind if they are long-callings or short-callings, but they are callings. I have no thinking in my head that it is a thing we need."

"These are deep thinkings," said Chooser, "and the women will go into near-sleep and the ever-minded will speak and I will choose. What is the three-twig?"

"The three-twig," said Talker, his voice rasping a little under the strain, "is the twig of Great Happening. When the two twigs are in the bundle and the bundle is strong then a three-twig will come to them. As I saw in the picture in my head the three trees and the three bushes covered in blossom, a great breath came through me and it was Her breath and it was a strong thinking so deep in the ever-mind that I could not break it open but I saw a not-woman standing by a fire; it came to me that he had not been chosen for many moons and that he was in deep-sleep, and suddenly blood poured from the mouth of the not-woman, and blood from between the legs of the not-woman, and I heard the words 'In my Womb were woman and not-woman, the chooser and the chosen, and they were the two halves of the one; now the halves are one and the one is of my Womb and will choose and be

41

chosen, and is woman and not-woman, the middle of the fire.'"

Talker paused. "That was the big twig of Great Happening," he said, "and the three-twig, and it is not for choosing, for it is a bird come flying from a moon to come, though I have no thinking which moon, but it will not be long. The talk is over for this dark."

"It is well," said the Chooser. "The women will gather and there will be a choosing for here are many broken twigs, but it does not come to me that the blossoms are big twigs broken, and it does not come to me that the three trees and three bushes are big twigs, and there is no great change in them. The three-twig we cannot choose. It is a moon to come or not to come and it will be happening or it will not." She nodded to the Caller. The Caller, looking across at Talker, rose to her feet also, almost as if to challenge his height.

"In Her Womb we lie this dark, and in our bodies She keeps Her presence," she said in a voice far louder than customary. Manka, on the very edge of the circle, bowed her head.

○

FOUR

"I have walked in near-sleep all this dark" said Manka, "I have walked up to the Womb and have entered the Womb and have seen the Change." She brushed her hand across her brow in weariness. Gron, seated cross-legged before her at the mouth of the cave, drew in his breath. Plara, crouching beside him, touched his hand. "It is a hidden thing that has come from the Womb," said Manka, "and there is loin-stirring in it and breath-ending and a great fire and new callings."

Gron felt the warmth running down his arm from the shoulder and his fingers tingled. He opened his fingers wide and looked at them. There was a mist around them like light upon stiff water in the great cold. He looked at Plara and around her head was the same mist. He felt a strength in him. He said, "I am an outer-thing. I am a not-woman and have been Taken. A strong thinking has been broken." He looked at Plara. "And I have a loin-stirring for Plara," he added boldly.

Plara reached out her hand and touched his. "I have been Taken," she said, "but it comes to me that I have a loin-stirring for Gron, and a strong thinking is broken and I am an outer-thing." Her eyes filled with tears. "Here are two outer-things," she said. "It is a big hurting."

Manka nodded. Her eyes were smudged with pain. "There is one Long-Calling that only the Taken may speak," she said, "and in the dark I made this Long-Calling, and it is a Long-Calling I give you now for it has come to me that you must Wander and this is the calling you must have in your mouths." She paused. "Hill-Builder, Womb-Filler, Reed-Breaker, Fire-Breather, Tree-Shaper, Fish-Swimmer, Deer-Caller, Change-Maker, Breath-Singer, Bird-Hurler, Wolf-Runner, Great Gatherer, dance in me the Dance." The words came from her as if it were another voice than hers that spoke them, a deeper voice, a more quiet voice.

"What is 'Dance'?" asked Gron, suddenly seized by a sharpness in his head.

"'Dance' is a hidden thinking," said Manka, "but from you it will not be hidden."

She paused. She said, "This is the happening. When the moon is full round the Talker will bring change and the change will be a great hurting on the Kindred and a great hurting in Her. At the big fire it came to him that the Talker wears a skin about his belly and that a not-woman who has not been pleasure-chosen for many moons will stand at the fire and that blood will spill from the mouth and from between the legs and it will be a Great Happening. In my long mind there are thin bags made of the inmosts of the giftings and they are filled with gifting blood, and one is in the mouth for the teeth to break, and one between the legs for the legs to break, and not one of the Kindred will see it for the mouth is shut and the skin is over the legs. It is a happening all who are Taken have in their minds for it can take away hurtings if callings are well made and from the deep-sleep. This is the Great Happening and. . . . "

Gron interrupted her. "Talker will spill blood and be Chooser and Caller and Talker in one skin bag?"

Manka nodded. "There is a bird-thinking I am sending," she said. "It is a bird-thinking no Taken one may send, but when a great hurting nears the Kindred; it is not a white bird or a black one but red, and I am sending it to Black-Haired Deer-Walker, and it will come to her to choose Talker, this full round that is near, and there will be no Great Happening to Talker, for there is a strong thinking that a not-woman cannot break the twig of pleasure-choosing, and that a not-woman who breaks that twig is an outer-thing and gone away from the Kindred."

Plara giggled. "That red bird could go to all the women and all choose the not-women that have not been chosen for many moons," she said. Gron chuckled.

Manka sighed. "To send the red bird out" she said, "is to make a hurting in me."

"And these two outer-things?" asked Gron, lifting up Plara's hand in his own. Manka frowned. "Plara will Wander," she said, "and it will be the thinking of the Kindred that she is Taken and the Taken Wander. You, Gron, will Wander. I will put a thinking in the Kindred that you lost a gifting and went to seek it and a thinking that there are wolves."

"How many moons?" asked Gron.

Manka sighed. "There is no thinking in me," she said. "It will come to you in the forest. It will come to you under a bush or in a cave or by a deep water.

"Go," she said, "when the Gathering is ended, and hold fast in you the great calling, 'Hill-Builder, Womb-Filler, Reed-Breaker, Fire-Breather, Tree-Shaper, Fish-Swimmer, Deer-Caller, Change-Maker, Bird-Hurler, Wolf-Runner, Great Gatherer, dance in me the Dance.'" Her eyes closed and she leaned back on the pile of skins in the cave.

Plara looked at Gron. "I will choose you this dark," she whispered. Gron squeezed her hand.

○

The man called Skang sat cross-legged in the highest fork of the big tree and let the pictures fill his mind. Through the thick bracken fronds he saw the village below him, a huddling of stone huts with roofs of mud and branches, the fire-pit in the centre of them, and the naked people. He saw not far away below him the round stone-walled place with the coloured creatures, some white, some grey, some mottled, some black, and the black haired boy with the stick that watched them and freed them after sun-start and put them inside again at sun-end. He saw the men with their small spears and their big spears, and the women and the small ones. He looked through the pictures and could not see a man with stag's horns on his head, or a big post with the skull of the wolf upon it. He could not see bows or arrows. He gnawed on his knuckle. These were not people of the Deer. He looked through the pictures once again. It was high sun. He felt the heat of it on his back, and there was a crow on the tree a leap away, black, head cocked, watching him. Should he give the crow to the Great Wolf? He felt for the bow at his side. Crow was small meat but small meat fills the narrow belly and it was five suns past that he had fallen on a deer and it had been a young one. He told himself, "No." The crow was looking at him with a bright eye. He made the sign of the Great Deer on his head, the spread horns and the hoof between them.

He looked again at the coloured creatures. Some were fat. Good meat. Fatter than deer. He felt spittle running and put berries in his mouth. He made a sound in his head for the creatures. The sound was "Unk." These were people of the Unk? He came to himself in the big tree and pictured again the three men that had walked beneath it at sun-start. They had not smelt him. That was another grass to weave into the mat. He had smelt them and lain still, but they had not smelt him. Were these people without smell? He pictured old Krill who, when the smelling had gone from him to the Great Wolf, was sent to the women and made to weave mats. He grunted to himself. He frowned. He pictured himself crawling again out of the woodland and round the big hill into the bracken above the Unks and at sun-high sending an arrow into an Unk and sliding down on his belly to take it away, the boy not smelling him. Then he pictured the Unks crying out. Unks could smell. He had seen their muzzles moving. He bit his knuckle once more. There were two pictures he could see; one was of the village tribe coming to him with the spear points to the earth, and with an old man offering meat, and one was of the tribe with spear points towards him and an old man shouting the wolf-shout. The pictures were in a mist. They were not people of the Deer but of the Unk. An old man held the skull of an Unk towards him, an Unk with horns from its mouth. There were Unks with horns from their mouths.

It was the highest sun. He closed his eyes. Words came to him and other pictures of a man coming into his village and of the bows drawn upon him and the old man standing silent. The stranger was given meat and a woman. The picture was blurred but the words were loud in his head. "In the Day of the Deer at sun-end none can be given to the Wolf."

The Day of the Deer? He pictured that Day, the great stag borne into the village, the stag with seven tines. He opened his eyes. He blinked at the high sun. He did not wish to see that picture, the big man running as he had run, not after sun-end in the wolf-time, but at sun-start in man-time; then the whistling of the arrows; the man at the edge of the woodland fallen; the old man binding deer horns upon the bloodied head, and deer hooves round the hands and feet, and after that the women with their knives.

He turned to another picture. It was of a man come into the village at sun-end. It was not a Day of the Deer. The man had a big staff with green leaves on it and there were leaves pinned with thorns to the skins around him. He struggled to hear the words the man had spoken. "People of the Deer, I feed the deer," he had said. He was given meat but not a woman. He was given a knife of horn and a bow and was called Feeder and made a member of the tribe. At the next Day of the Deer he was told to pick a woman, and now Feeder was part of the tribe. The pictures faded and as they faded he heard himself saying "Unk people, I feed the Unk," holding out roots? leaves? crawling things? He slept.

○

Fleay could not get the picture out of her head. It was not a thinking but a happening. It was not a happening she wanted. The face was the face of Talker. She sat down under a bush, her reed basket of berries beside her; even in the shade, and the day soon to be taken, she was sweating. She put her hand upon her fur-hole and rubbed gently. The picture did not go.

"It must be a good pleasure-choosing this dark," she told herself, "a two-choosing." She giggled. There was a thinking that a woman could two-choose if she had not made birth for ten moons and Fleay had not made birth at all.

"I will two-choose," she told herself, "or three- or four-choose," she said, though there was a deep thinking against that. "Deep thinkings are twigs to be broken," she told herself. "Talker has broken many twigs." The face of Talker grew bigger in her head. "Talker breaks thick twigs," she mused. "He puts his thinkings into the Chooser and his callings into the Caller and he is the Watcher of the burning. It is my thinking that Black-Haired Deer-Walker who is Back-Hurting Eye-Burning Berry-Picker this day could be chosen Long-Sleeping Fire-Maker." She thought of herself as Fire-Maker, one of the three strong bushes at the gathering. "Talker will put big blossoms on that bush," she told herself, "and I will put a thinking in him that the blossoms..." She could not think of the blossoms and set the matter aside.

"Fire-Maker does not pick berries, or make with reeds, or scrape skins, or gather fish, but makes fire only," she told herself. "At the full round of the moon Talker will put the thinking into Chooser and I will be Fire-Maker. She giggled again. "Chooser and Caller and Fire-Maker have the first choosings," she told herself. "I will not choose Talker when I am Fire-Maker. I will choose...." " and she pictured the not-women of the Kindred one by one. The light was growing fainter now, and heaving a great sigh she took up her basket. "I will choose Talker," she said. "It is a good happening," and, rested, her step springy, her shoulders straight, she set off back to the village.

○

Chooser looked round the gathering. "This is my choosing," she said.

Gron and Plara at the outermost edge of the circle glanced at one another, their eyes wide, their lips a little parted. This was a big happening, but not the great happening that would follow for them.

"Talker has had a thinking, and a happening, and it has come to him that there should be three standing trees at the gathering and three bushes at their feet, and that the trees should be Chooser, and Protector and Talker and the bushes should be Caller and Maker and Fire-Maker. There is no strong thinking that women and not-women cannot stand at the gathering. Talker has given the trees blossoms. There is no strong thinking about that. I have chosen that there shall be these three trees with their blossoms and these three bushes. I have chosen."

As she stood up there was a murmur around the gathering.

"Come, Talker," she said and he, rising, came to her and stood at one hand, tall and lean.

"Come," she called to Protector and he stood at her other hand. Caller, Maker and Fire-Maker came from their places and squatted in front of the three.

"Bring the blossoms," said Chooser in a clear loud voice, and first a woman brought a cap of pigskin to Maker and he put it on his head, and then a woman brought a great loop of vines with dried leaves upon them and laid them around Fire-Maker's shoulders. A third woman gave Caller the skull and the bones of a crow upon a thong and she placed it around her neck. Protector smiled as the necklace of wolves' teeth and bears' claws, which he himself had made, was hung upon him. Talker was given his staff, which was a handspan higher than himself, and a deer skin was wrapped around his belly and tied with thongs. The last blossom of all was a feather necklace and a crown of feathers, and these were put upon Chooser.

Chooser spoke again, "The trees and the bushes have their blossoms," she said. "It is a strong thinking for this moon and all moons."

There was silence in the gathering. The firelight flickered over the seated ones, and the standing ones who seemed taller than woman and not-woman had ever been before, and over the tallest thing in the gathering, the staff of Talker. Talker cleared his throat. His mouth was dry. He felt a warmth in his body that was not the warmth of the fire.

"Dry twigs have broken and new strong twigs have been bound in the bundle," he said. "In Her, Through Her," he added, lifting his voice.

"And it has come to me that he who will spill blood from his mouth and blood from between his legs and who has not been chosen for many moons, being woman and not-woman in one body, will bring a great happening before the full round of the moon and will be a great tree."

There was a hiss of sound in the gathering.

"How great a tree?" asked Pingar. "Greater than the three great trees that are Chooser, Protector and Talker?"

Talker moistened his lips with his tongue. "That is hidden within Her Womb," he said, "and the birth-making is to come."

Manka spoke. "You have a thinking I am not of the Kindred, Talker," she said, "and that is a thinking that has not been chosen."

She lifted her hand and pointed at Chooser. "I am not a tree, but a cavern," she said, "and the Womb is a cavern from which all things come and to which all things return. Is the Cavern of the Kindred?"

Chooser hesitated. Talker spoke quickly. "The basket that holds the berries cannot be a berry," he said.

Manka lifted her chin. "Without the basket the berries are scattered," she said.

Talker held his staff high. Necks craned to see the height it reached.

"There is a happening in me," he said. "I see the not-woman standing in his blood, not pleasure-chosen for many moons by woman, bed-sharing with none, long-minded and ever-minded from many moons of

49

near-sleep. I see him enter the cavern, both woman and not-woman, and there is a greater basket than ever before."

He drove his staff down to the earth with a great thump. Chooser, before another word could be spoken, said, "This is a deep thinking and it is a happening to come. Is the talk over?"

"It is over," said Talker.

"It is well," said Chooser, and Caller, in the sudden stillness almost whispered, "In Her Womb we lie this dark, and in our bodies She keeps Her presence," and a low murmur of talk began as the food was brought.

Talker sank thankfully back upon his heels. It had been a good gathering. Chooser had followed the track he had made in her thinking. He smiled to himself, his face shadowed from the fire that Fire-Maker was even now replenishing. He should have been Taken, he reflected. He had the way to move the the thinkings of others on the tracks he chose, and at the full round of the moon, standing taller than all, he would begin to speak and there would be the blood from his mouth and from between his legs. . . .

His reverie was interrupted. It was the woman Fleay. When he was—what would it be called? Cavern-Holder? Womb-Keeper? that was it—Womb-Keeper! . . . and could choose like a woman, she would be in his hut that dark . . . what was she saying?

"Make a loud hearing," he said testily, "I was in near-sleep for three or four breaths."

Fleay raised her voice. "Talker," she said clearly, above the murmur of conversation, and using, for once, the full formula, "In Her, Through Her you are chosen."

Talker gaped at her. "No," he said, "No."

Fleay felt a sudden surge within her, a great laughter, and raised her voice farther, using words she had never had need to use before, "Not-woman, I choose you and you are chosen or you are an outer-thing. This is the strong thinking In Her, Through Her and of the Kindred. Speak!"

Talker could not speak. He tried but the words would not come. Fleay, excitement rising in her, opened her mouth for the third saying, and there was a silence in the gathering.

"Not-woman, I . . . ," she began.

Talker bowed his head. There was a pain in his chest and a sickness in his stomach. "I am chosen," he mumbled.

Fleay suddenly giggled. "A long-minded man may have a long pleasure-thing," she said aside to those around her, and there was laughter. Talker gazed past her into the fire.

"Womb-Keeper," he said to himself and the calling was a puff of smoke in the wind. Fleay took his hand.

"We will eat and then pleasure," she told him, herself gazing into the flames. "Fire-Maker," she whispered to herself and it seemed as if the fire blazed more brightly.

From the very edge of the circle Plara and Gron stole away, and as soon as they were in the darkness they held hands. "I choose you," whispered Plara, and "I am chosen," said Gron, and Manka on the far side of the circle bowed her head and sent bird-thinkings of the colour of the yellow flames out across the Gathering to speed and ease the Wander they had begun.

○

FIVE

Fleay turned over on her bed of skins and jabbed a finger into Talker's ribs. He was dark-sounding louder than Kraw could caw. He choked, grunted, turned over. Fleay stared up in the blackness of the hut. It had not been the strongest pleasuring of all, but it had been different. At the beginning she thought he had a hurting. He looked as if he would make eye-water, and he had shaken as a reed shakes, and the pleasure-thing had been soft worm. She giggled to herself. Soft worm had soon become bending twig, she reflected, feeling it once more in her hand, and then thick twig, fur-hole filler, and Talker was not Talker but Mouth-Bruising, Breast-Biting, Spear-Plunger, and it had come to her that he was a big fish in a net, leaping, a fish in her womb leaping, and she must draw him to land.

She shuddered suddenly. She had a picture of a great fish too heavy for her to hold, but then there was another fish on the grass and she was standing upon it as Chooser had stood at the Gathering, and the fish was moving still as her toes dug into it. She turned over. She would choose him this coming dark and the dark that came after it; after that she would not choose him for three darks, and then she would choose him again and the net would be tight around him. There was a thinking that no woman could choose the same not-woman every dark, but Talker was Talker and he would make a strong thinking that it could be done. She would keep him as Wet-Mouth Quick-Walker kept a bird in her reed cage, as moons ago Small-Haired Berry-Treader had kept a short-minded twig-legged deer until it was fat for meat. She felt a loin-stirring, but it was a different hotness, like the hotness for the big gifting, not like the hotness for Thick-Armed Spear-Hurler.

She said, to herself, surprised, "I am making long-callings this dark." She tried to say "Harn" but the short-calling was stone in her mouth. "It is a dark for long-callings," she told herself. "It is a dark for strong thinkings. I am ever-minded this dark." She reached out to the body beside her. It was not soft worm but bending twig. She took it between her finger and thumb.

"You will have big pleasuring," she told it, and then, suddenly, into her head came another picture; it was of a red bird and the bird was in her hand, struggling to be free. She held the bird and would not let it go. The bird opened its beak to cry, but could not. She gripped it tightly and the struggling ended. Cautiously she opened her hand. The bird was no longer there.

"The bird is in me," she whispered to herself. She lay back on the skins and frowned. "Not one dark and two and three," she told herself, "but many darks and moons."

Talker groaned in his sleep. Bending twig was becoming stiff twig. She giggled.

"Black-Haired Red-Winged Loin-Stirrer," she whispered to herself, "and Chooser," she added, pushing herself against the slowly wakening body at her side.

○

Manka, cross-legged in her cave, stared out at the grey light of dawn. Her eyes were bloodshot, her breath laboured. There was a pain below her breasts and her arm ached. Heavily she lifted her hands and put them to her head, making wings of them, and closed her eyes. She sent out a calling. *Red Bird, Red Bird, come, come, come,* but there was no picture in her head. She stood up, spreading her legs, planting her feet firmly upon the packed clay of the cavern floor, and spoke the words aloud, "Red Bird, Red Bird, Red Bird, come!" Sweat stood out on her forehead. She knelt down, her thighs splayed as if to give birth. She pulled in her belly. She made the words deep and strong.

FIRES OF THE KINDRED

"Red Bird, Red Bird, Red Bird, come! In Her, Through Her, this Calling: Come!"

A picture came into her head. It was of a red bird flying away from her into the forest and as the bird entered the forest the trees became flames and the fire spread from tree to tree until her head was filled with the picture of it. She dropped her hands into her lap and opened her eyes.

"The red bird comes to no calling," she told herself, "and there will be hurtings in the Kindred." She rocked backwards and forwards on her heels. "It is a heavy happening I carry now and carry to breath-ending," she whispered, "and it is a great Change that comes In Her Through Her."

Her arm ached more than ever. She crawled to the pile of skins and lay down, tears shining on her cheeks. Outside the cool wind of early morning rustled the bushes, and the grey light in the sky turned red as the sun slid up from the horizon.

○

The clear moon of late summer, now on the wane, slid through a wisp of cloud as Gron, lying on his back beside the fire, stared up at the sky. Plara, her head nestling into his shoulder, her body cradled by the crook of his arm, was fast asleep. Gron's arm was stiff, but he did not move it, though the fire was dying down and he knew he must add more of the wood he had gathered from the fallen tree and the dry dead patches of the bushes. He made pictures in his head, fitting them together one after another slowly and carefully so that the last picture would not come too soon. He saw the Gathering fire again, small and far away, as he and Plara went into the woodland; he saw the skin bundle where Manka had hidden it in the big bush beside the crooked tree; he saw the hands of Plara spinning the fire-stick, the little wisps of smoke, the bent head and pursed lips over the tiny glow, the flicker of yellow, the small twigs taking up the fire, and then the warmth and the red light on her thin face, on her outstretched hands. He took a deep breath and saw the meat, the berry cakes; and then the last picture overcame all the others. He closed his eyes the better to see her wide eyes shining in the half-dark under the moon, her shadowed throat, her parted lips, and feel again the strong pleasuring that was somehow also a near-sleep and ever-minded as if, for the space of a wolf-cry, he had been Taken all over again.

He twisted his head and stretched his neck to look down at Plara. His arm tightened around her. She gave a small snuffling grunt like a young gifting. He looked back at the moon. "In Her, Through Her," he said to himself, and then "In Her, Through Her, this pleasuring." He paused. "It was a deep pleasuring," he said, "and I have a thinking that it was deeper than a pleasuring. Other-Gron and Other-Plara were in it. It was Other-Pleasuring. In Her, Through Her," he added and then as the half-moon slid from the last wisp of cloud and he craned his neck once more and saw the woman's sleeping face, "The pleasure-choosing was the breaking of a twig, but the Other-Pleasuring. . . . " he paused at the new calling, tasting it in his mouth, both sweet and bitter.

"This Other-Pleasuring," he whispered to himself in awe, "is a wind that will blow down trees."

○

Skang lay behind the great stone on the top and looked down at the creatures in the walled place. The half-moon was bright and the sky clear. The boy was not to be seen, and the small fire near the stone huts looked very small. He began to crawl down the slope. He would use a knife, not an arrow. He would pick out a small fat one and cut its throat as quiet-mouthed as a wolf that runs alone.

He put the knife between his teeth. The metal was bitter on his tongue. *Great Wolf,* he murmured inside his head, *grant me this Unk that when I come to you I will be strong.*

He inched himself slowly up to look over the wall. He crawled round the wall to the opening. It was blocked by branches bound together with thongs. He eased it open a little way, wincing as the briars to one side of it raked his shoulder. "Blood for the Wolf brings meat to the man," he muttered under his breath.

A small fat Unk lay before him. He bent over it, grabbed it round its belly, and slit its throat with one slash of the knife. There was a piercing gurgling shriek that astounded and terrified him so that he almost dropped the thing. He reeled back through the opening, stumbling into the briars, blood pouring over him and over the briars and the stone beneath them, and ran up the hill. There was a shout from the small fire below him by the huts but he was too far away for even the strongest bowman. Soon he would be in the woodland. He dropped over the brow of the hill.

"Blood" he thought suddenly, "Blood. The blood will bring them to me when the night is done."

The river did not run this side of the hill; he could not break the trail that way. He stopped by a boulder to think it out. He had a sudden picture of Bleng, the horned one, standing at the mouth of the Cave of the Wolf where the body of Binnen had been laid, and of the mark he made upon the stone when it had been moved back into place before the opening.

The voice came to him again. "Here I make the death mark of the Deer that none of the people may enter this place," and he had made the mark on the stone with blood of the deer. It was a mark of power. None could pass, but the Great Wolf himself in His mist-shape and even He in His mist-shape only.

"Skang is not Bleng," he told himself, "but he knows the mark," and with his bloodied hand he drew on the rock the shape of the antlers pointing downward, and said aloud, for the Great Wolf to hear, "this is the door to the place of the Great Wolf that none may pass." He wondered for a second or two if he should have made the mark of the Unk, but he did not know it. He tried to make a picture of it in his head, but there was no picture. He slung the dead creature over his shoulder and ran steadily down the hill towards the woodland.

○

Plara stood still as a tree at the edge of the little clearing. She closed her eyes and sent a bird-thinking out over the trees. *I am sweet grass. I am a small clear pool. I am untrodden grass. I smell of sweetness. I am a cool pool. I am grass for deer. I am a pool for deer.* She felt the bird descending, down past the bushy tops of the trees, past the shining branches, and saw the deer. It lifted its head and sniffed, its nostrils wrinkling, its mouth open. One forefoot moved restlessly. *I am the sweetest grass. I am the clearest pool. I am In Her Through Her.* The deer trotted into the trees. Plara breathed more deeply. *You are coming to me. You are coming to me. You are coming to me.*

Gron, spear at the ready, stood beneath a tree at the side of the clearing. His eyes shone. He breathed slowly. He sent his smell away into the treetops. He took on the smell of leaf and grass after rain. He emptied his head of every picture but that of the deer. There was the crack of a breaking twig, the rustle of leaves. The deer trotted into the clearing, and stood still sniffing the air. Its antlers quivered as it bent its head to graze.

In Her, Through Her, In Her, Through Her, this that is Hers to give us.

He leaped and struck, and the spear swerved in his hand and drove through the throat so hard that the point came out the other side. Plara raised her eyes up to the sky and called out in triumph, "Hill-Builder, Womb-Filler, Reed-Breaker, Fire-Breather, Tree-Shaper, Fish-Swimmer, Deer-Caller, Change-Maker, Breath-Singer, Bird-Hurler, Wolf-Runner, Great Gatherer, dance in me the Dance." Gron, already kneeling by the deer that kicked weakly as the blood pulsed ever more slowly from the red wound in the throat, looked up at her. His head filled with a picture, and it was Plara and not Plara, it was Plara but it was also a deer and the deer had a wound in its neck and flowers were falling from the wound.

○

Harn stood tall in the grey dawn and looked at the dried blood on the entrance to the gifting place. Talker, Chooser, and Manka stood beside him.

"It was not wolf," he said. "I see no wolf marks. It was an outer-thing."

Talker, heavy-eyed, nodded. "My head is an empty bowl," he said, "I have no thinking."

Chooser frowned and turned to Manka. "Is it an outer-thing?" she asked, her voice troubled.

Manka crossed her arms across her breast. "I am not of the Kindred," she said. "Protector had that thinking. Is it a strong thinking?"

Chooser hesitated and looked towards Talker. He said nothing. She took a deep breath. "It is not a strong thinking," she said.

Manka smiled. "It is an outer-thing and it is not an outer-thing," she said. "It is wolf and it is not-wolf."

"That is a twig I cannot break," said Chooser sharply.

"There is blood upon Her face," said Manka, pointing to the carved stone half hidden in briars, "There is blood from Her eyes and it is Her eye-water."

Chooser took a step backwards. "The trail is warm," said Harn impatiently. "I will take two not-women and will follow it."

Chooser nodded. She looked again at Talker. He did not speak. "Harn follows the trail," she said with nervous decision, "and at the Gathering there will be strong talk." She turned and went down the hill.

The stone face, bare to the sunlight, the briars pulled away, stared out with bloodied eyes.

○

Deep in the woodland, their faces dappled with the leaf-shaken light, Plara and Gron examined the entrails of the deer. "I am not Manka," said Plara nervously, "but Manka is in my head and there is a picture of a great stone and there is blood upon the stone." She peered more closely. A mist drifted across her eyes and through the mist she saw a tall figure. "It is a not-woman," she murmured half to herself and half to Gron, "and there is blood on his body and there is a black-haired woman." The mist dissolved and she blinked and shook her head.

Gron closed his eyes and held his hands over the tangle of wetness. "I am touching a fish," he said. "It is a big fish but it is not cold. It is warm like a gifting. And it is making a loud breath."

"I hear the loud breath," said Plara, suddenly excited. "It is a loud hearing and it is a hidden thinking and the hidden thinking is from the ever-mind and it is... far from me," she said, "far, far from me."

Gron rocked back and forth upon his heels. His eyes rolled upward in his sockets. The hair on the nape of his neck bristled. He made his hands into fists. His voice was deep and hoarse. "Go far," he husked, "Go far," and his body went slack and he gave a huge sigh and then another and opened his eyes.

Plara stared at him. "In Her, Through Her, this thinking." Gron nodded. His mouth was dry.

"Far," said Plara, "Far?" Gron nodded once more.

"It is the Wander," he told her, "It comes to me that a small stone has rolled down the hill and that big stones will follow."

CAMROSE LUTHERAN COLLEGE
LIBRARY

Skang lay by the woodland pool and rubbed his full belly. The sun was high in the sky and the wind still. He had run along three small streams, once up-current and twice down, and he was now deep in the woodland. "No man followed the trail," he told himself. "The death-mark of the deer is a wall that none can pass." He moved a picture into his head and again saw the huts and the small fire. He put another picture in his head and saw the men and women come from the huts towards him, and he heard his voice, "People of the Unk, I feed the Unk." He had leaves pinned to the skins around him.

Another picture broke in upon that one. It was a picture of men with spears and the spear points were lifted and the men were coming closer. He opened his eyes and stared into the pale blue sky. A movement in the top of a tree touched the edge of his sight. Very slowly he pulled his bow to him and fitted an arrow. "The strong deer eats each leaf," he told himself, narrowing his eyes, and cautiously rising to a sitting position. The movement in the tree top quickened and a big crow was suddenly beating its way high up over his head. He threw himself flat on his back and shot the arrow straight up into the sky; the black wings stopped and the crow fell like a stone into the pool, transfixed by the arrow. Skang grinned to himself and sprang to his feet. "It is a wolf-word," he told himself, "and the word is good." He waded into the pool. The crow floated to the surface, its black wings outspread, its beak agape.

○

Plara and Gron watched the crow beating its black way across the sky. "There is a hidden thinking of Kraw," said Plara meditatively, and even as she said the words the crow gave a little jump and twist in the air and fell from the sky.

They stopped and turned to each other. "It is a bigger stone," said Gron. "Kraw is small but it is a bigger stone."

Plara closed her eyes. "A picture comes to me," she said, "and it is of a spear in Kraw."

"No hand of the Kindred, not even of Harn, made that spear throw," said Gron.

"It was Her hand." Plara said firmly, "The Wander goes on many tracks and this is one," and they turned in the direction of the place where the crow had fallen from the sky.

○

Fleay stared into the pool; it was dark and still and her Other stared up at her. Then, "I have a red bird in my breast," said Fleay to her Other, "and in my hands and my mouth and my fur-hole and it is a strong bird."

The face in the water wavered, blurred, and then became clear again. Fleay said softly, "Strong thinkings and strong happenings come to me from the long-minded one I pleasure and in near-sleep. I am ever-minded." Her voice rose a little. "There is a happening that comes to women at a Watching Pool, and here at this Watching Pool I am Black-Haired Red-Winged Loin-Stirrer and I am Chooser and I am making a loud calling to the happening."

She paused. The face in the pool became darker. Three dead leaves, brown as bark, slid over the face and the leaves were two eyes and a mouth and there was a redness of fire in the eyes and the mouth was black. Fleay, legs apart, feet firm upon the earth, felt a great heat moving up her legs into her belly and through her breasts into her throat and head and down her arms.

She swayed. "It is the warm," she whispered. Her eyes closed. She was walking through the huts of the Kindred, and first one of the Kindred would meet her eyes and then another and the eyes did not see her, but became her eyes, and the hands her hands. She felt herself sliding into a darkness, and the darkness was around her like a cloak of heavy fur. She took a deep breath, throwing her arms wide, and the cloak slid from her shoulders. Then the darkness came again and it was a great cold and she cried to herself, "Red Bird, Red Bird," and the cold was gone. She stood in the middle of the group of huts, waiting.

"The one and the two," she said. "The three comes," and suddenly a great wind drove up against her and she swayed to the wind as a tree sways, her toes digging hard into the earth, her hair flying about her.

"Red Bird!" she shouted into the wind and the wind dropped. The huts and the Kindred were no longer there and she was standing beside the pool. She looked down into the pool. No face looked up at her. She shuddered and then suddenly giggled. "The fish breaks through the net," she said and turned back along the track through the trees. On the crooked branch of a tree a crow looked down at her. It opened its beak. Fleay spat on the earth and the crow made no sound, but rose clumsily into the air and flew high up into the sky. Fleay smiled. "Red Bird, Red Bird," she whispered, and putting out her hand to a dry bush she broke off a twig and held it for a moment looking up at the now distant crow. Then, her tongue between her lips, she snapped the twig in two.

○

Harn, wearing his necklace of teeth and claws as Protector, stood tall at the gathering, the firelight reddening his body. Beside him Chooser in her feather headdress seemed small and Talker, for all his great staff, seemed less imposing.

"I followed the trail," said Harn, "it ran down the far steep of the hill, and it was a quick running for there were two or three paces between the blood marks, and the runner was a not-woman for his footmark spoke to me from a flat stone in one place and from bare earth in another. It was a not-woman and an outer-thing."

He stared challengingly across the fire at Manka. "The trail ran to a great boulder and there was a pool of blood at the boulder's foot and on the boulder there was a mark in blood. It was a mark like a forked branch with the fork at the top, or it was the mark of legs, and in between the legs there was a small hump. It was the mark of the hump on a woman's fur-hole or of a man's pleasure-thing when there is deer skin on it." He paused. "I had a thinking, and it was a deep thinking, that this was trail-ending. Broon, Krank, Flod, had this deep thinking that was mine. We looked at the mark and there was a hurting in us. It was the hurting that happens when a big deer is coming quick with big horns and the spear is gone. Broon, Krank, Flod had this hurting that was mine. That is the calling of it."

There was a moment's silence. Chooser said, "Is there a thinking in the Kindred?" Fleay said, "It comes to me that Talker had a picture in his head. It was one who was a woman and not-woman in one body, and who spilled blood from the mouth and from between the legs. The blood-mark on the boulder is a mark of legs and the legs are woman and not-woman, and there is blood on the great stone face that Maker made."

There was a longer silence. "Maker has a thinking?" queried Caller.

Maker spoke slowly, his voice thin with anxiety, "I had a thinking it was Her face, but this thinking came to me when the making was done. I had a picture of the stone and of a making coming from the stone. The face looked at me when the making found ending and I had a deep thinking that it was Her face."

"Is this a stiff twig?" asked Caller. "It is a bending twig. I have no strong thinking."

Fleay spoke again. "The stone face is the mouth with blood on it; the blood-mark on the boulder is the legs with blood on them. This is the picture that came to Talker, and this is the Great Happening before the full of the moon, and this is the great Tree.

Caller nodded. "Talker?" she said, and again, "Talker?"

Talker lifted his staff and struck it on the earth once, twice, and a third time. He felt a surge of confidence and again a warmth in his body that was not the warmth of the fire.

"Black-Haired Deer-Walker holds a straight spear," he said, "and Thick-Armed Spear-Hurler has the fish in the net." There was a gasp at the use of the long-callings. Talker did not hear it. "It comes to me that She came into Maker and in his hands She made the head. It comes to me that She came into the outer-thing and in his hands She made the legs. It comes to me that the head should be set upon the legs and the great tree stand at the Burning Place, and that the Burning Place be Her place and a fire be made there for burnings and for Gatherings at the full round of the moon and Gatherings She chooses. It comes to me that there are two fires. The one-fire is the hut fire, and at the hut fire there will be eating and drinking and pleasure-choosing at the coming of the dark. At the two-fire in the Burning Place there will be no eating and drinking, but Burnings and Great Gatherings and there will be a wall about it, and there the great Tree will stand."

There was a murmur among the Kindred. Manka spoke quietly. "This is a Changing, and a great Changing. I am ever-minded and I have the strong thinkings and the hidden thinkings within me. I have been Taken and I have Wandered ten-and-five times. I am long-called Fire-Handed Breath-Changer, and I am the basket that fills with berries, the cavern that is Her womb." Astonishingly, she stood up. Talker drew his breath in sharply. The Kindred sat still as stones. "I see the great Tree that comes to Talker and it is a stone upon a stone and its leaves are stones and its flowers stones and its berries stones, and I see the Kindred standing under the Tree and the stones are falling on the Kindred and the blood that is on the stones is the blood of the Kindred, and there is a great hurting in Her womb."

Talker lifted his staff. "I am ever-minded," he proclaimed, "and it comes to me that the hurting in Her womb is a birth-hurting, and that the stones that fall are Wet-Skinned Breast-Nuzzlers and the blood on the stones is the blood of the Kindred that fills them, and that the stones are the stones of tens and tens and tens of huts for the tens and tens and many tens of Kindred. It comes to me that the Great Tree eats the breath of the great fire and makes loud callings and the Kindred hear with a strong hearing, and the Kindred are strong and have no hurting."

Manka stared at him across the fire. Still standing, she folded her arms across her breasts. "The loud Kraw is the hungry Kraw," she said and, letting her arms fall to their sides, she turned and left the Gathering.

Chooser waited a few moments. None spoke. "The women will gather," she said, "and we will be ever-minded and at the full round of the moon I will choose. Is the Talk over?"

"It is over," said Talker. "It is over for this dark."

"It is well," said Chooser, and Caller, her voice both harsh and nervous, said, "In Her womb we lie this dark and in our bodies She keeps Her presence." The men left the fire to get the meat. The young women fetched the bowls of drink. Fleay, eyes shining in the firelight, went up to Talker.

"Talker," she said softly, "I choose you this dark."

○

The dawn was cold and the sky grey as Gron and Plara left the small fire and followed a deer-track down the slope through the trees and bushes and came upon a pool in a big hollow. Plara dropped to her knees.

"I was Taken by a pool," she said, "and it was in a Watching Pool I saw Gron and had a loin-stirring for him. It was then Kraw gave me a deep thinking and I saw the twig breaking. This is not the one-pool or the two-pool. It is the three-pool and there is a black feather floating in it." She shuddered.

Gron said, "It is another stone down the hill," and went to the water's edge. Plara followed him. Together they looked into the water. A little wind was scuffing the surface but as they watched the wind dropped and the water was still. They looked down into the water, and between their two faces looking up at them the black feather floated like a crevice in rock. Plara felt a sudden cold move through her and then a spreading warmth. The feather grew before her, widening, until it was a cavern in a hill-side, deep, unfathomable. She peered into the cavern and deep inside it she saw two red eyes looking back at her. She drew her breath in sharply and the eyes vanished and there was nothing but a black feather floating over the eyes of the face that looked up at her.

"It is a cavern," she whispered, "and there is a wolf in the cavern."

Gron grunted, only half hearing her; he was holding his hand out over the water, the fingers spread, and he was looking past his fingers at the feather. "It is a knife," he said, "and it is not of bone and it is not of stone and it is cold as the stiff water when the branches are bare."

Plara took his hand with a convulsive movement and the wind rose again and ripples spread across the two reflected faces. As they watched, the feather spun slowly round and round and then drifted away out over the pool. They walked round the pool's edge and Gron knelt and studied the grass. "An outer-thing was here," he said, "woman or not-woman, and it ate." He picked up a bone and sniffed it. "It ate gifting," he said, and then, picking up feathers, "It gave breath-ending to Kraw."

Plara nodded. "We must follow," she told him, "and it is far."

○

Skang frowned and scratched himself. He was deep in the woodland and farther still from the people of the Unk. He put the picture of the Unks in his head but it melted away like dawn mist. He put a picture in his head of the men of Unk with their spears pointing down to the ground and then towards him, but the pictures changed into water and went away. "None follow me," he told himself, "and the Unk was good meat." The words rang hollow as an empty bowl knocked against a tree. "What follows then?" he asked himself, and the picture came into his head as quick as an arrow, and it was a great black wolf. He opened his eyes to shut it out and changed his position in the fork of the tree.

"Great Wolf," he whispered aloud, "I give you the leg of the deer I will kill," and for a moment felt comforted. He stood up on the tree fork and looked out over the woodland. Blue-hazed in the distance he could see hills mounded smoothly as woman's breasts. "Woman," he said to himself and felt the disturbance in his loin. He put a picture of a woman into his head, a woman in her cloak of thick bear skins, and then, the skins falling from her, a woman naked, a woman lying on the bearskin cloak, smiling; but as he watched the picture, his pulse quickening, his flesh thickening, the woman was no longer a woman and the darkness of the bearskin was the blackness of a cavern and two red eyes were watching him from the darkness. Sweat started up on his forehead. "What is the law I have broken?" he almost shouted, and he saw again the crow falling from the sky. With sudden energy he grabbed his skin bag, pulled out the dead crow, threw it down from the tree, and then followed it; breathless, caught up in an urgency and a terror he had no name for, he began running through the woodland, letting his body take what direction it would.

○

Talker, crouching, scratched a picture in the dust with a dry twig. "The wall will be here, and here, and here," he told himself, "the fire here, and the Great Tree will be here. Here I shall stand, and here will stand Pranda and here Grek, and there the Kindred." He hesitated. He rubbed the drawing out with his heel. Fleay, a little way apart, watched him.

○

Plara crouched down by the dead crow. "The hole through it is a hole through the heart," she said, and, putting her finger into the hole in the breast, she held the bird up on her thin finger, moving it up and down so that the wings shook as if attempting flight, though the head hung down and the blood-encrusted beak gaped at the earth. "It holds a hidden thinking still," she said, "and it comes to me that we must take this thinking and only then will it rest in Her womb."

She held the crow high above her head and, as they watched, the head lifted, the gaping beak snapped shut, the wings rose, flapped and spread wide and the bird soared upwards, its wings growing longer and broader: it was no longer a crow but a black eagle circling above them,

66

spiralling higher and higher, and as it rose they could see that it held something in its talons and that it was a huge rock. Necks craned, they gazed upwards and the eagle let go of the rock and it came falling towards them. With a cry Plara let her hand drop and leapt to one side, and Gron jumped back. Between them on the earth lay the dead crow.

Plara took a deep breath. "We will burn it and then sleep," she said and she turned away to find wood for the fire. Gron picked up the crow curiously and then, putting it to one side, scrabbled in the grass upon which it had lain, his fingers digging into the grass roots.

"Here," he said, holding up a round pebble clear as water. "Here!"

Plara, spinning the fire-stick, nodded. "It is a birth-egg," she said, emotion drained from her voice, "Manka had a thinking that it would come to us." She threw twigs on the tiny fire. "Have you a picture of the Kindred?" she asked suddenly.

Gron tried to put the picture in his head but could not. "No, there is no picture."

Plara nodded again. "Put the crow on the fire," she said, "the Kindred are gone from us and the birth-egg has come."

○

SIX

On the mud at the edge of the river there was a clear footprint. "Outer-Thing was in this place," said Gron. He looked for another print and found it. "He followed water in its running," he said, "and did not cross to the other side."

Plara said, suddenly, "There is a thing of black in my picture and it is Bear."

"The tree," whispered Gron, and, slinging the hide bag over his shoulder, he climbed the tree, whose thick branches stretched over the water, and Plara followed him. Plara sat in the crook of the tree holding the birth-egg in her hand, and staring into it. The sun, dancing through the leaves, struck a small spark within it, a flicker of white light, and as the light widened she saw a black feather falling from the sky and growing larger and larger until it was as big as a man. It fell with its quill downwards, straight as a stone, and the point of the quill was a stone spear point. Then the picture dissolved and the light shuddered and was gone.

She looked at Gron. He was lying belly down on the big bough overhanging the river's edge and his spear was in his hand. She could tell from the way his body tensed and slackened that he was taking away his smell. She closed her eyes and took away her own, breathing in leaf-smell and wood-smell and breathing it out again until she felt herself a part of the tree and yet not a part of the tree but the shaft of a spear, her body glistening like smooth bark in rain, her back straight, stiff, and strong. Gron raised himself slowly and stood up on the broad branch, his toes down-turned to keep a firm grip. The hide bag swung gently from a smaller branch beside him. He reached into it and took out the black crow feather and put it into his hair. Plara sighed with pleasure. "The water is in the bowl," she told herself, "and it will not spill."

The bear, black as the blackest dark, shouldered through the bushes and lumbered onto the river bank. It raised its muzzle, snuffling, then lowered it to the ground. Its shoulders were humped with fat, its eyes small and hard as the sharp brown pebbles in river pools, its fur glistening in the sunlight. Almost delicately it padded along the shore, its rump swaying from side to side, and when it was under the tree it turned towards the river edge, its muzzle twitching softly as it bent its head to the water.

Gron held the spear in front of him, the point of it between his feet. He took a slow deep breath, stepped sideways off the branch, and to Plara it seemed as if he stood upon air before he dropped upon the bear, the whole weight of his body on the spear that now jutted down two handspans below his feet. The spear drove into the bear exactly behind the skull and the two feet followed after. The bear pitched forward, rolling sideways and roaring, the red mouth scattering spittle and sudden blood, but Gron had leaped to one side and rolled clear. The bear tried to get to its feet but could not. Its head swung from side to side; its claws scrabbled at the mud, raking great weals into the earth; it roared and the huge bulk shuddered and lay still.

Gron, on his feet again, let out a whoop, the cry of the Kindred at a kill, and then "In Her, Through Her!" he cried, and "In Her, Through Her!" Plara responded, coming down from the tree. Together they looked at the huge mound of fur.

"It is Her meat," said Plara, "and Her warm in the cold that comes," and she raised her eyes up to the sky and called out in triumph, "Hill-Builder, Womb-Filler, Reed-Breaker, Fire-Breather, Tree-Shaper, Fish-Swimmer, Deer-Caller, Change-Maker, Breath-Singer, Bird-Hurler, Wolf-Runner, dance in me the Dance."

Gron bowed his head. The black feather in his hair trembled to a sudden breath of wind.

○

Sitting cross-legged by the fire in the cavern, Skang pulled the arrow from the shining fish. He stared out of the cavern's mouth at the roaring thundering sheet of water. "Wolf will not come here," he told himself. He gutted the fish with his knife, pierced it with a pointed stick, and held it over the fire. A twig cracked, and two sparks flew out and landed on the earth before his feet. They looked like two red eyes.

○

"The water is loud and the air is cold," said Gron, pulling the bearskin more tightly round him. Plara, curled up in her own robe, grunted.

"When dark has gone we must follow the fall of the water down the steep," said Gron. "It will be the full round of the moon in two darks," she said, "and we must make long-calling. What long-calling shall we make for Gron, for Gifting-Herder With Black Eyes?"

Gron smiled. "Black-Eyed Bear-Slayer? Strong-Backed Woman-Pleaser?" he suggested. He stared up at the moon. "And the outer-thing? Is there a long-calling for the outer-thing?

Plara put her two thumbs to the side of her head and made wings of her hands. "I send out a bird-thinking and it comes back to me and it tells me Spear-Flying Wolf-Runner. I see a spear small as a reed and quick as a deer leaping; I see a knife that is the red-brown of dried blood and that is not stone; and I see two eyes and they are the eyes of a wolf."

"We have heard no wolf," said Gron. "We have heard no wolf in all these darks on the Wander."

"It is the ring I make around us each dark," said Plara, "and the fire that I fill with spear and knife and shouting."

"Not one wolf-cry, not one," said Gron.

"In Her, Through Her this good," Plara murmured, and then, sitting up, "It is not Spear-Flying Wolf-Runner. It is Wolf and not-Wolf. It is the wolf that runs and the deer that runs from the wolf. It is the cry beginning and the cry ending. It is Taken and not Taken."

She began to tremble. Gron put his hand upon her and sent warmth through his hand. "Sleep," he said, "Sleep."

○

It was dawn before Skang discovered that he had left his knife in the cave. He sat on a rock by the river and the picture of the knife lying on the brown earth came to him, and then a picture of the two red eyes and the pain of the sharp rocks and the sharp arrows of the chill water on his back as he leapt down through the edge of the waterfall and stumbled onto the other bank of the river. The moon had been almost full. The moonlight had been bright, but cast deep shadows, and he fell many times before, half crawling, half wading, he reached land. His legs ached and there was dried blood on his knees. He heard again the voice in his head, the Wolf-voice that filled him with fear. "Meat for the Wolf," he murmured to himself, "meat for the Wolf is strength in the man" and, rising stiffly to his feet, made his way up the bank and into the trees. "Deer, Deer, the Wolf is calling!" he said inside his head. "Deer, Deer, the Wolf is hungry." He moved slowly, often pausing, lifting his head, sniffing the air, peering, his bruised hand fastened tight around the spear.

○

"He was in this place," said Gron, raising his voice against the hush and roar of the falling water. He stirred the edge of the cold wood-ash with his foot. "Fishbones," he said, and then "Knife." He bent to pick it up.

"No," said Plara suddenly. She crouched down by the knife and stared at it.

"Not of bone and not of stone," she murmured, "and it has come from fire." She closed her eyes.

"A picture comes to me of a big fire, and of heavy stones of two colours and they are changing to water, and then the water is a knife shape and there is another water and water-smoke and the sound of rock hitting rock—not rock hitting rock in the stone-finding place, but rock hitting rock in a big cave where there are two hearings, the one hearing near and big, the two hearing in the air and far." She held her hand out over the knife. "There is the hand of a not-woman that has a hurting. It is the hurting that comes from a thinking of breath-ending. There is a cutting of thongs. There is a running. There is blood. The blood is the blood of a deer and the blood of a gifting."

Gron squatted beside her as she opened her eyes. "It comes to my hand," he said, "but it turns in my hand and is driven into me. In my blood it becomes a pleasure-thing and it is in your fur-hole. I smell the breath of a wolf." He pulled his fingers back, with a sudden gasp.

Plara stood up. "In one dark it is the full round of the moon," she said, "and in the shining of Her moon we will see and in Her near-sleep we will have pictures in our heads, and we will take away this hurting." She took a crow feather from the bag and scratched a ring around the knife where it lay on the earthen floor of the cave. "We are in Her womb," she said. "The shouting water is the water of birth-bringing. At the full round of the moon this hurting will be gone and the knife of the wolf-runner will be the knife of the birth-helper. That is the change that comes to me."

Gron nodded. "The ring is a strong wall," he said. "It will not be broken. There is meat in the bag. I will get wood," and he went to the mouth of the cave and stood there dark against the brightness of the falling water so that Plara had to narrow her eyes to see him clearly.

"Leaves that make fire-breath for the full round of the moon," she said, "and three round stones." Gron turned and as he left the cave she gazed round the cavern and "In Her," she said, and again, "In Her, In Her."

○

Very slowly Skang dragged himself to the base of the big tree, his hands clutching at grass clumps, his one useable knee pushing him forward. He gritted his teeth to stifle his groans. At the bottom of the tree he rested his back against the rough trunk. The light was fading. He tried not to picture the great deer with the wide-spreading many-pointed horns that had come at him from the bushes with a crashing of leaves louder than the sound of the falling water at the cave, but it came into his head again and again, as did the vanishing tail of the smaller deer as it leapt out of the clearing, with blood on its shoulder.

He had a picture of the spear in the air, and of the deer turning just as it struck, and the spear glancing away. Then, once more, came the picture of the huge lowered head, the horns, the savage pain in one leg as he crashed backwards and the loud crack as the other leg, twisted beneath him, snapped like a dry twig. He pushed his back up against the tree. The blood was still running down the gashed thigh but less strongly now. The thong that he had tied above the wound bit into the flesh but was stopping the blood. He pushed the foot of the wounded leg hard against a humped root of the tree and slowly stood. There was a thick branch a little above his head. He reached upwards with both hands, letting all his weight rest on the one leg, and grasped the branch.

"Strong! Strong!" he told his hands and arms; he tightened his muscles and pulled, at the same time thrusting down on the bleeding leg. His head and the upper part of his chest were over the branch. He wrapped his arms round it, and held on.

"Back be strong," he said in his head, and "Leg be strong." He swung side-ways, first one way and then the other, and then, pushing his body further over the branch with his hands, he swung the good leg up and over and lay breathless, the hard wood pressed into him. Ahead was the first big fork of the tree. He pulled himself towards it, stopping at every breath. Below him in the now quickly fading light, he could see the bow and the skin bag. He could not see the spear. It lay beyond the bushes in the clearing.

At last in the fork, he leaned his back against the trunk, and pulled his useless leg round until it lay across a bough and no longer hung down. He closed his eyes. The picture of the big deer came into his head again, its great spread of horns, its face, its eyes, and the eyes that were the eyes of a wolf. He shuddered. Reaching up, he fumbled at the thong on his shoulder which held the arrow bag. There were two arrows left in the bag; the rest had fallen out. He unloosened the thong and, reaching behind him, passed it round the trunk of the tree and tied it in front of him. Now if sleep came to him he would not fall. He tested the knot. It was firm. A picture came into his head of a man crawling through the trees, eating berries from the bushes, and then of a man lying still beside a bush and a black crow watching him. He spat at the crow and it melted away, only to reappear on another bush.

He closed his eyes. He would put a picture into his head of a strong man walking through the trees, a strong man with a big spear and a bow and a sharp knife. He saw the knife lying on the cave floor beside the fire. He opened his eyes. Over the trees the full moon was rising.

○

Plara stared at the rising moon. At the cavern's mouth a jutting rock split the falling water into two great torrents and the moon rode up the clear sky in the space between them. "It is Her moon," said Plara softly, "It is Her moon and it is through Her, in Her, and it is Her speaking."

She sat cross-legged before the fire and gazed across it at the moon. Gron sat a little way behind her.

"There are three callings," murmured Plara, "and the one-calling is Woman before choosing," and she threw a handful of wet leaves upon the fire; the fire spluttered and smoke rose up and for a moment the moon was staring through the smoke.

"The two-calling is Woman at birth-bringing," said Plara, and she threw another handful of leaves into the fire and the smoke grew thicker.

"And the three-calling is Woman long-minded and birth-helping," said Plara, throwing the third handful of leaves, "and the one and the two and the three are the days and darks that have gone; and the day and the dark that are here; and the days and the darks that come."

She paused. The moon, through the drifting smoke, wavered, and changed colour; it was no longer the pale yellow of the little spreading flowers of the time of new growing, but had many colours, and around it stray drops of the falling water flashed and glittered. As the smoke drifted away a sudden gasp of the wind swept a fine mist across the gap between the torrents and every colour was there, in the shape of the round belly of a woman lying on her back before birth-bringing, or the shape of a man's back bending to pull a fish from the water; then, as suddenly as it had come it was gone, and the moon was clear again, riding in the far far sky, shining more yellow than any flower.

Plara's eyes were unseeing now. She said aloud, "I open the eye that is Her eye," and it came to Gron that a beam of light as straight as a spear flew from the moon and pierced Plara in the forehead. As it did so, Plara, in near-sleep, picked up one of the white stones.

"It is in the boughs of a tree," she said, "and there is blood on it and there is a great hurting. This is the one-stone; the two- and the three-will come."

She laid it down and took the second stone. "Kraw is sitting on the back of a wolf," she said, and shook her head as if puzzled, putting the stone aside.

She held the third stone a long time, and then, her lips scarcely moving, breathed rather than spoke, "Come to us Mother that we may come to You."

The stone fell from her hands and she rocked back and forth on her heels; her eyes closed and then opened and she said in a voice that was deeper and huskier than any Gron had heard her use before, "Her strength is in my hand and my hand is Gron's hand and it blesses the knife."

Gron looked at the knife. He put his hand out to it and picked it up. It was warm in his grip. He held it up against the huge round of the moon and "In Her, Through Her," he said.

Plara, in the new deep voice said, "Here are the callings," and she stood up, her arms stretched out, her legs apart, her belly thrust forward, the firelight reddening her legs and thighs, the moonlight washing her jutting breasts and upturned face.

"In this full round of the moon I call Black Eyed Gifting Herder and new-call Knife-Handed Black-Winged Bear-Jumper."

Gron bowed his head. "The calling is In Her, Through Her," he said. "In this full round of the moon I call Twig-Thin Stiff-Walker and new-call Moon-Eyed Skill-Maker; this calling In Her, Through Her."

She swayed a little. The hair on her head moved suddenly as if a wind had touched it, or as if it were the ruff of a wolf before battle.

"In this full round of the moon I call One-Leg Wolf-Runner. In Her, Through Her is this calling and to Her he comes."

She let her arms fall, and stood still and stiff as a winter tree in the windless morning, staring out at the moon, and for the first time since the Wander began, over the roar of the falling waters came the cry of a wolf, once only, cutting through the air in answer.

○

As the sky lightened over the mounds of the far hills, at first soft grey and then streaked palest yellow, Skang stirred. He had slept at the last, after the big moon had gone down, and pictures had come into his sleep one after another, pictures of broken branches, of wolves waiting in a ring around him as he leaned against a big stone, and pictures of fire that were more than pictures, for the fire burned and spread into his chest. There was a fire in his chest now and his breath was loud and scraped inside him with the sound of a dry twig scraping against stone. He moved his wounded leg cautiously. It was stiff. His other leg he dared not move. He looked down. Beneath him lay the skin bag, the bow, and scattered arrows.

"The wolf with three legs eats late," he told himself grimly. He untied the thong that fastened him to the tree. He pictured the way he must fall. The good leg must hit the ground first of all, then he must fall forward, roll over on his shoulder. He looked across at a small tree. It was straight and strong. He pictured the knife cutting the tree and making a staff.

The picture went away. He saw the knife lying on the floor of the cavern. He leaned back against the trunk of the tree. There was a thing to say. He closed his eyes and hunted for a picture of Bleng, the horned one; Bleng was standing by the fire, his hand uplifted. He was speaking in a high voice. "Great Deer, Great Horns, give us meat. Great Wolf, red-eyed, hurt us not. Great Deer, Wide Horns, fill our bellies. Great Wolf, knife-toothed, starve us not. This I speak for the People of the Deer, and this I give to the belly of the Great Wolf."

The two upraised hands came down, and there was a piece of meat in each of them. Bleng threw the meat into the fire.

"There is no meat in my hand," Skang said in his head, "and there is no fire. And the Great Deer came to send me to the Wolf and the Wolf is waiting."

He shuddered, and then, suddenly, he saw the full moon as he had seen it in the darkness, and thought he heard, as he had heard then, the harsh cry of a crow.

"I sent the crow to the Great Wolf," he told himself, "but it is in the air." He looked up through the tangle of branches to see the crow but saw nothing. A blackness came over his eyes. He put out a hand to push it away but it would not go. He was swimming in deep water and the water was over his head and his chest was tight and more tight. He lunged upwards to the surface, but the surface moved away higher and higher above him. He was the crow in the pool. There was a hole in him through the chest. His wings were broken. He opened his mouth to cry out but the cry would not come. He gathered all his strength. The blackness was everywhere. He felt strength move into the broken wings. He lifted them wide and thrust himself forward. He was no longer in the water. He was in the air. There was wind on his face, and then a flash of light and a flame that ran through him like a spear and a great blow. Then only the darkness.

○

77

Gron looked at the man lying beneath the tree. "We have followed and found," he said. "It is a not-woman and an outer-thing and its leg is broken under it. It is One-Leg Wolf-Runner." He looked around him and picked up an arrow. "This is a small spear," he said, "and it has bird feathers. It is the spear that flies." He picked up the bow. "It is a bent bough," he said, "and there is a thong on it." He frowned, curious, and squatted by the body. "It comes to me," he said, "that this is not yet a breath-ending." He looked up at Plara.

"It is a beginning," she said slowly, "and the beginning must be in Her womb." Gron gently rolled the man over, straightening the two legs and the arms, and now the face was staring sightless at the sky.

"It comes to me," he said, and warmth spread down from his shoulders into both his hands and he spread his fingers and put his thumbs together and his hands were wings moving gently above the face of the hurt man.

"Wake. Be still. Speak," he said, "Wake. Be still. Speak."

The man's eyes opened. They stared up at Gron. There was hurt in them.

"You are One-Leg Wolf-Runner," Gron told him gently, "and a branch that does not move in the wind."

The man moistened his cracked lips with his tongue. "I am going to the Great Wolf," he said, "and you are the crow that waits for the gifts of the Wolf."

Gron frowned; the words were twisted and rough to his ear. "You speak as a bough creaks," he said.

The man coughed. Spittle flecked the corners of his mouth. "Kill me," he said. "I have run and I have fallen."

Gron made his hands move over the face once again. "You are in near-sleep," he said, "In Her, Through Her, and you will do my thinking that is Her thinking."

The man's eyes closed. Gron turned to Plara. "It comes to me that it will walk to the cavern with a branch under its shoulder and its arms upon us," he said. "It will walk in near-sleep, and we will be given strength to bear it over the rocks into the cavern, and then... " His eyes clouded.

"And then," Plara said softly, "One-Leg Wolf-Runner will be in the Womb and Two-Leg Wolf-Runner will come from the Womb with

Kraw on its back, and it will be not an outer-thing but a strong not-woman."

Gron took the dark knife and found a straight young tree. Plara took up the arrows and the bow. The man on his back under the tree lay still, his eyes closed. Plara shuddered.

"It is Change," she whispered softly, "It is Change."

○

SEVEN

Skang's fingers gripped the thick fur of the beast under him. He was riding the beast, belly pressed to its back, and the forest through which he was riding was on fire. He could hardly breathe. His chest was cramped. There were thongs round his chest. He was tied to the beast. He cried out. A voice came to him, a woman's voice. There was something at his mouth, something hot and sour, a drink that ran down his throat making a clear passage through the forest so that the smoke that choked his chest dwindled and he could gasp and gulp at the air.

The bear was moving more slowly now, walking steadily. The thongs were looser. The voice came again. The woman was walking beside him. She was making words and the words were white birds and he was no longer on the back of the beast but in the air and swimming through the air as if it were water. The air smelt of green leaves and wet grass and was filled with the roar of falling water.

The words were pictures. There was a picture of a bundle of twigs and he was one of the twigs. He was also a feather, a black feather, spinning down from the sky. But the feather went away from him and he was looking into a deep pool. The mask of a wolf looked up at him, red-eyed. He leapt back. There was a fire in front of his eyes, a fire as big as man, and the man held a spear. He crouched down in the bracken and breathed in leaf-smell, breathing deeply, deeply, and the man of fire was gone and the pool was there again. He crawled to the lip of the pool. The mask of the wolf was no longer there. It was a woman's face. Her lips were moving. He heard the words. They were not pictures but words. The words were "Sleep," and then again, "Sleep," and "Sleep." He closed his eyes on the face. He was a feather again drifting, drifting, drifting.

○

"The fish is good," said Plara, staring at the three poles thonged together over the smoky fire and the big fish swinging there. Gron, cutting the skin away from the new-killed deer, grunted.

"Deer and fish and berries," he said, with a touch of pride in his voice, "and the barks and the leaves: the great cold will bring no belly-hurting."

Plara nodded. "Wolf-Runner will hunt again when the moon is gone," she said.

Gron frowned. "He is in near-sleep and in full sleep from day-making to dark," he said, "and through the dark. Is change coming?"

"I am putting the strong thinkings into him," said Plara, "and he comes to Her. He comes with a slow step. He sniffs the air and his head turns this way and that. There are new smells. In Her, Through Her he comes."

Gron looked at her. "This is more than Manka," he said. "This is Her in you."

"It is the birth-egg," said Plara. "I look and I see; I listen and I hear. It is Her. It is also Manka. I have a picture of Manka but not of the Kindred."

Gron closed his eyes. "I have a picture of a gifting," he said, and was silent.

○

Skang, seated with his back to the wall of the cave, stared down at the two lengths of branch thonged round his leg.

"I will walk?" he asked.

Plara nodded. "In three darks you will stand; in ten you will walk."

Skang sighed. "You came to me in sleep," he said.

"In sleep I came; in near-sleep I came; I brought you into Her womb."

82

Skang nodded. "There are words new as peeled sticks," he said, "and you gave me those words."

"Speak them," said Plara, smiling. Skang flexed his good leg. He would walk in ten nights. In ten 'darks', he corrected himself.

"I was a man," he said slowly, "a man of the Deer and the Great Wolf."

He shuddered a little. Plara's eyes were on his eyes.

"In this place I am a not-woman and the Great Wolf is gone and I am in Her." He blinked. He said hesitantly, "There is no death."

"There is breath-ending," said Plara, "and going back into the Womb, and there is change in the Womb and breath-beginning."

Skang said, "This is good."

"In Her, Through Her," said Plara.

Skang spoke carefully. These were new words. "A picture comes to me," he said, "and it is a picture I see through the fire-breath. It is a picture of Gron and of Plara and they are two, and a picture of Skang and he is three and one, two and three are in one hut. Can a woman have two men, two not-women? A not-woman has one woman that is his woman." He paused. "That is my strong thinking," he said, almost triumphant at the word.

Plara spoke gently. "A picture comes to me," she said, "It is a picture of a woman. It is light-ending. She chooses a not-woman for pleasuring. At dark-ending the not-woman goes away. That is one-dark. It is two-dark. The woman chooses a not-woman. It is not the one-not-woman but the two-not-woman. The woman chooses. The not-woman is chosen. In Her, Through Her this strong thinking."

"There is fire-breath on the picture still," said Skang, "but it drifts away. If I were a man," he said very softly, his eyes dark, "and a walking man I would choose you."

"You are a not-woman," said Plara firmly, "and you do not choose."

Gron looked across the cave at Skang and then at Plara. "He is still Outer-Thing," he said.

"He is the wolf on which Kraw will ride," said Plara, "and a thick twig in the bundle. Put meat in the fire," she added. Gron did so.

○

Gron leaned on his spear underneath the big tree. "The earth water is stiff and shining," he told himself. "The great cold is coming." He stamped his feet and, looking down, admired the deer-skin foot-holders he had made. He had come a long way from the cave, his head filled with a picture of round shining nuts as big as the paws of a hare, and now, in the high sun of the day, he had found them lying under trees whose leaves hung down like the spread hands of a woman blessing, but bigger than the hand of any woman or not-woman. Some of them had escaped from their wombs that had split open. Some still in the womb hung in the tree, the green becoming brown. He lay down the spear and began gathering. After a while he beat the branches with his spear and more fell. He moved from tree to tree, the hide bag heavy on his shoulder.

He would spend this dark in one of the big trees, he told himself, and then a picture came into his head of the cavern and of Skang and Plara. Skang was walking. He was walking in the cavern, leaning on a spear, each step slow as the step of a long-minded white-headed not-woman near to breath-ending. He stopped again under another tree. In a hollow at its root the earth-water was no longer stiff. He knelt and stared into the dark pool. Another picture came to him. It was of Plara. She was looking at Skang. It was near dark. She was making words. He looked at her lips.

The word was "Choose."

Plara was choosing Skang. He felt a hurting in his belly. He said to the pool, "In Her, Through Her," but the hurting did not go away.

"It is the strong thinking," he told himself. "A woman does not choose the one-not-woman every dark, and the strong thinking is from Her and is good. Plara broke that twig with Gron. She chose Gron dark after dark after dark. She is mending that twig."

The hurting still did not go away. He looked deeper into the pool. His Other looked up at him. His Other's mouth was down-turned, and there was eye-water on its cheeks. He felt tears on his own cheeks. He sat back on his heels and sent a bird-thinking out to Plara. It was a black bird-thinking. It was sharp as a spear point. He said, *Plara, Plara, Plara*; and then he turned the bird in the air and sent it up into the empty sky.

"In Her, Through Her," he told himself in a strong voice. "In Her, Through Her." He smeared his tears with the back of his hand.

"It is Change," he heard in his head, "It is Change."

○

Skang leaned heavily upon the spear and gazed into the fire. "Gron short-calls me Outer-Thing," he said, stumbling a little over the words, "and Plara calls me not-woman and I am One-Leg Wolf-Runner."

He looked across the fire at Plara. "There is a picture you do not see," he said. "I looked on a not-woman and the not-woman found breath-ending. I looked at a great deer and the deer leapt into the big water and was gone. I looked at the woman I was pleasuring and she made birth and the wet-skinned breast-nuzzler did not find breath and there was a hump on its back. There was a strong talking and I became an outer-thing to the People of the Deer."

He paused and shifted uneasily on his feet. "I have no calling for it," he said, "but the people had a calling for it. It was Wolf-Eye." He said, "I am Outer-Thing Wolf-Eye."

He bit his lip. "It comes to me," he said, "that this calling has not gone away."

Plara said gently, "One-Leg Wolf-Runner came into the Womb at the full round of the moon. Ten and ten-and-five darks have come and have gone. In three darks or four it will be the full round of the moon and there will be new callings."

She lowered her eyes from his gaze. Her hand fumbled as she knotted another thong of the net. She said, "There is another thinking in you. You have put a mat of reeds upon it. There are reeds between me and the fish. Shall I put my hand through the reeds?"

She looked up, sitting very still upon the bear robe. Her eyes were bright. Skang turned his head away. "Look!" said Plara. He looked. Her eyes were the colour of the fire.

"Wolf-eyes," he whispered, "You have the red eyes of the Great Wolf."

He backed away, clumsily, to the wall of the cave. His breath was coming in big gasps. There was sweat on his head and on his chest. His whole body was hot.

Plara said, "They are the eyes of One-Leg Wolf-Runner and a picture comes to them. It is a picture of a fur-hole and there is a pleasure-thing in the fur-hole and there is a woman with blood on her breasts and on her mouth."

Skang dropped the spear and slid down the cave wall. His knees would not support him.

"It is a picture that will not go away," he said. "It is a picture and a hurting. In the dark my pleasure-thing is a stiff branch and I have a great loin-stirring."

Plara nodded. "The fish is in my hand," she said, and lowered her eyes.

Skang felt the heat leave him. He shivered. He said, "Do not look at me with wolf eyes. They burn."

He said, "Do not look at me!"

Plara laid aside the net and stood up. She stared steadily at Skang. She raised her right hand and made a round shape with thumb and forefinger and gradually made the hole smaller until there was no hole at all. Skang moaned with pain, his hands clutching his groin.

"It was a bad picture," she said. She stared into his eyes.

"It is a hurting," he gasped, "It is a bad hurting." He forgot the new words. "You are killing my woman-plunger," he shouted, "You are killing it!"

Plara lowered her clenched fist and spread the fingers wide. "The hurting is gone," she said. "If the bad picture comes to you this dark the hurting will happen. It will happen till the dark that you are pleasure-chosen."

Skang whimpered with relief. "I will be chosen?" he whispered, "I will be chosen?"

Plara sat down on the bearskin and picked up the half-knotted thong. "For every cry there is a hearing," she said, "and for every pebble a place upon the earth."

O

Gron, curled in the big fork of the tree, pulled his bearskin cloak round him and stared up at the riding moon. His head was filled with pictures of Plara. "There is a hurting in my belly," he told himself, "and it will not go away." He saw the face of Plara as she slept under the moon on the first night of their Wander.

"There is pleasuring and Other-pleasuring," he reflected. "Plara and Gron have Other-pleasuring. Plara and Skang . . . "

The knot in his belly tightened. He gritted his teeth. "Woman must pleasure-choose," he said firmly, "and not-woman be chosen."

He changed his position in the tree. The picture of a gifting came into his head. It was huge and hairy with stained yellow tusks and its eyes were red. He stared into the red eyes and the eyes stared back. He could not move. His arms and legs were heavy and stiff. He mumbled helplessly, "In Her, Through Her, In Her, Through Her.... "

Very slowly the picture blurred and faded and again he was staring up at the moon.

○

"It is a bow," said Skang, "and these are arrows. There are two arrows. We must make more."

Plara and Gron, seated on the river bank, watched intently. He fitted an arrow to the bow-thong and drew the bow.

"It flies straight," he said, "and strikes hard."

He let the arrow go and it sped through the air and drove into the trunk of a big tree.

"Bring it back," he told Gron. Gron went to the tree. He pulled hard on the arrow. It was firmly fixed. He took a deeper breath and pulled again and it came into his hand. He ran back.

"It strikes deep," he said, "and in a breath."

Skang smiled. "It kills quickly," he said, and then, remembering, "It sends breath-ending quickly." He paused. "Kill is a good calling," he said, "I will say kill. It kills deer and birds and hares... "

"And Kraw," said Gron. His face felt stiff.

"And Kraw and ... not-women," said Skang. "We must make a bow for Gron and a bow for Plara," he added quickly, "and tens and tens of arrows."

Plara gazed across the river. Her eyes were hard as pebbles and her breath came quickly. She crossed her arms on her breast.

"It is Change," she whispered, "It is a wind that blows down trees. I see a not-woman and a deer and the not-woman has a spear in his hand and the spear strikes the deer and the deer falls. The deer and the not-woman are one and one; they are in one bed. I see a not-woman and a bow and a deer. The arrow flies in a breath. The deer falls. The not-woman and the deer are not in one bed. They do not touch." She shuddered. She said very softly, "When the bringer of breath-ending and the one that ends breath are not in the same bed.... " Her eyes clouded. She shook her head. "The picture has gone," she said, "but I am cold."

Gron held out his hand for the bow. Skang gave it to him. Gron held it in the way Skang had held it. He fitted an arrow to the thong and drew the bow. He let the arrow go and it sped through the air past the tree into the bushes.

"It is a straight-flying bird," he said, "It is a bird-spear." He smiled happily. "It is good," he said.

○

Plara leaned against the inner wall of the cave and gazed at the curtain of water through which the moonlight shone. Gron at one side of her, Skang at the other, stared. Her face was expressionless, stiff, her eyes wide, unseeing. She took a deep breath. "In Her, Through Her, this full round of the moon," she said, her voice a croak, and then, stepping from the wall towards the fire, threw off her cloak of furs and stood naked. For all the cold in the cave, warmth flowed into her. She crossed her arms upon her breasts, slowly, deliberately. Her lips moved.

"Breath is taken," she said, and then, throwing her arms out wide, "Breath is given."

Her hands fell to her sides. Leaning back on her heels, she spread her legs and thrust her belly forward so that the fire flickered red upon the inside of her thighs and upon the dark clustered hair.

Her voice rose. "It is the hour of calling. I make the callings. . . . "

Skang shuddered and pressed himself against the wall behind her. The voice, which was not Plara's voice, grew louder, "I am Her, in Her, through Her, the twig that is green, the bough that is cut, the staff that is made."

She paused and shook her head from side to side, her long hair seeming to float in the air.

"I am the knife moon, the full round of the moon, and the moon that is eaten by the dark."

She lowered her head. A sudden puff of smoke rose from the fire and was coloured by the light through the falling water and there were many colours. She cried out then, in a great cry, "Here is the one that is called and it is Breath-Taking Wolf-Runner, and it is chosen."

Skang, sweat beading his forehead, gave a gasp that rasped his throat.

"Here is the two that is called, and it is Breath-Giving Kraw-Thinker, and it is chosen."

Gron's knees trembled. He opened his mouth to speak but could say nothing.

"These are the two, the one-choosing and the two-choosing, and they are the two legs of the Wander, the two hands of the making, the two eyes of the seeking In Her Through Her and they are of the Womb."

With the last words her voice dropped, and her body began to sway. Gron instinctively moved forward to catch her. Skang reached out his arm and restrained him. Together they waited. Plara was now swaying backwards and forwards, and from side to side, her head tossing, but her feet immovable on the cavern floor as if they were rooted there. The water's roar filled the silence, growing louder and louder. The smoke of the fire drifted away. The light faded. Plara sank to her knees, picking up the birth-egg from the earth before her. She hunched over, staring into it, and, in a voice much more like her own, said very quietly, "There is a great cold and birth-beginning; there is a Wolf and a Kraw and a white bird." Her voice grew even quieter, so that Gron and Skang could hardly hear it. "Hill-Builder, Womb-Filler, Reed-Breaker, Fire-Breather, Tree-Shaper, Fish-Swimmer, Deer-Caller, Change-Maker, Breath-Singer, Bird-Hurler, Wolf-Runner, Great Gatherer, dance in me the Dance."

They lifted her from the earth where she had fallen, the birth-egg still in her fist, and wrapped her in the cloak of furs and laid her between them. Then as the sun rose, one by one they coupled with her as if in a dream, and when the light was full they had no picture of which coupled with her the first, but only the sound of her voice that said not "You are chosen," but "She has chosen," and the warmth and the smell and the feel of her in their arms.

○

EIGHT

As the first gentle snow came sifting down from a grey sky Maker looked down at the stone between his knees. "It is a not-woman," he told himself, wondering, "and it has two faces."

He blinked and looked up at Manka. "A not-woman," he repeated, "and there is a one-face and a two-face and the one and the two are one."

Manka said, "Talker has two faces but these are not the two faces of Talker."

Maker shuddered. "A red bird came into my head," he muttered, "and the bird was in this hand, and in this hand, and the stone made its own shape. It was a bird-thinking."

Manka bent over the stone and put her hands upon it, one hand on each of the faces. She closed her eyes. "It comes to me that this is breath-taking and breath-giving," she said, "and it is a calling from Her; it is the coming out of the Womb and the going into the Womb."

Maker frowned. "That is a twig I cannot break," he said, "I will bring it to the Gathering by the great fire for it is the full round of the moon."

Manka nodded. "There is a great fire this dark," she said, "and Talker will stand before the Face; on his one hand will be Chooser and on his two hand will be Protector, and Maker and Caller and Fire-

Maker will be seated at the fire. There will be fire-breath and loud hearings, and this one-and-two face will be set upon a rock beside Her face and the rock will be a big rock."

She turned away. Maker looked up at her. "It is Change?" he queried.

"It is Change," said Manka. She looked out of the stone hut through the sparsely falling snow at the cavern on the hillside. "When the womb is empty the womb dries," she said, "and Manka is not of the Kindred." She spoke very quietly. She said, "There is a white bird and a sudden burning, and the burning is... " Her voice faltered. "I have no picture of the burning," she said, "The fire-breath is white and thick as mist."

Maker pushed the carved stone roughly to one side. "I make In Her, Through Her," he said, "This that I make is not of my hands."

"It comes to me," said Manka, "that our hands are reeds that move in moving water and some are broken."

Maker looked down at his hands. "They are not broken," he said. "Will they be broken?"

"Yes," said Manka. "They will be broken."

○

Plara lay still between the two men and stared up at the roof of the cavern.

"It is the great cold," she told herself, "and in the great cold the flowers hide in Her womb." She patted her belly. "There is a flower in my womb," she told herself and then, quickly, for she felt the familiar disturbance, "Be still! Be still!"

She crawled from between the two men and added wood to the fire, crouching over it. "The fire in the womb," she said to herself, and then, looking up at the entrance to the cave and the frozen curtain of the waterfall. "In two moons the stiff water will run; in three moons there will be flowers, and in eight moons there will be a birth-bringing in this womb."

She frowned and passed her hand over her eyes. "Not here? Not in the womb?" she questioned.

A picture came into her head. She was standing by another fire, a big fire. Her belly was swollen and taut. On one side of her was Gron and on the other Skang, and there was a loud shouting in her ears.

"Not here," she affirmed.

Her belly heaved. She pushed the little clay pot into the edge of the fire to warm the drink she needed.

"Leaf and bark, leaf and bark, heal all hurting, heal all hurting," she murmured. Gron stirred in his sleep. The pale light of late morning shone through the curtain of ice.

Sipping the drink, she brought the picture of the fire back into her head. There were two big shapes of stone there. The one-stone had a face carved on it, and it was Her face. It was the stone from the gifting place. The two-stone she could not see clearly. She searched for more pictures. They would not come. The smoke of the fire drifted across the big stones. She swallowed the last of the drink and sat back on her heels. She was suddenly very cold. She sent a small bird-thinking across the cave to Gron. He stirred in his sleep once more and woke.

"You have seen a picture?" he said.

"It was the Kindred," said Plara. "There is a hurting in me"

Gron stood up and came to her.

"The Wander has ending?" he queried.

Plara stared into the fire. "There is no ending," she said, "The Wander will not end."

○

"It came to me from Her," said Talker, standing beside the stone face and looking across the great fire at the rows of the seated Kindred.

"It came in deep-sleep and in the fire-breath which is Her breath. It is a strong thinking."

He paused.

Chooser cleared her throat. "I am Chooser," she said, "I and the women will choose."

"There are thinkings that are too strong for choosing," said Talker, "and these are the strong thinkings from Her."

Chooser bit her lip. "What is the thinking?" she asked.

Talker lifted his staff and drove it down on the earth with a thud. "It is a loud hearing," he said. "In Her fire-breath came the picture of the Kindred that came from Her womb, and the Kindred are two. There is a woman and there is not-woman. Stone Woman is here, made by Her hands through the hands of Maker. Where is Not-Woman?"

He pointed to the two-faced carving lying beside him on the earth.

"Here is not-woman," he said, "made by Her hands through the hands of Maker. In the picture I saw the one-stone that is Stone Woman and beside it the two-stone that is Stone Not-Woman and they were the two side-stones of the door of the hut that is Her dark and Her cavern and Her womb. I saw the picture and it came to me in deep-sleep and in the fire-breath that there are two stones at the Gathering, and woman and not-woman are the two side-stones of the hut opening."

He struck his staff once again on the ground. "This is the strong thinking," he said, "and there is no choosing."

There was a rustle of whispers among the Kindred.

"Talker does not choose," said Bode. "Chooser makes the strong thinking, and takes the thinking to Caller. Then Caller brings it to the gathering and makes it a loud hearing. This has been for tens and tens and tens of moons and is from Her." She drew in her breath sharply.

"It is Her breath, Her strong thinking," said Talker simply.

Bode wriggled uncomfortably. "Has Manka a picture?" she asked and turned around and looked over her shoulder at Manka seated alone at the very back of the Gathering.

"Manka is not of the Kindred," snapped Fleay from the very first row. "Manka does not choose. She has been Taken. She takes away hurtings, but she is not of the Kindred."

Talker struck his staff again on the earth. "Through Her, In Her, this breath and this strong thinking," he said.

Chooser pulled her big fur cloak around her. For all the heat of the fire, she felt cold, and there was a hurting in her head as if a thong were tightened around it. "The women will gather," she said, "and the women will do a thinking and the ever-minded will tell what they see and we will all be ever-minded for a time and I will choose."

Her voice trailed away. The thong around her head was tighter still. "Is the talk over?" she asked.

"It is over," said Talker, "It is over for this dark."

"It is well," said Chooser, and Caller, her voice husky, said, "In Her womb we lie this dark, and in our bodies She keeps Her presence."

A few flakes of snow drifted down, turning pink in the fire glow as they flurried gently upward over the flames. Manka rose heavily to her feet and left the Gathering. Fleay looked at Talker. His eyes were upon her. For three moons she had chosen him. She would choose him one moon more she told herself. In one moon she would hold within her all his thinkings and happenings. His long-mind would be hers.

She looked at the picture in her head, the dark pool, and the face of her Other in the pool and felt again the warmth in her body and the tight thongs binding her and the breaking of the thongs. She made a bird-thinking and sent it straight as a spear to the place between Talker's eyes. She did not say "I choose." She rose to her feet. She would eat and drink and go to her hut and he would follow.

○

NINE

Skang sat over the hole he had made in the ice and gently joggled the thong that stretched from his fingers down through the black water. Plara crouched beside him. "This is woman-thing," said Skang crossly, stretching his still stiff leg. "A not-woman hunts with spear and knife and bow."

Plara stroked his shoulder. "In one moon or two the wolf will run again," she said and then, "I will bring the fish."

She closed her eyes and held her hands in front of her, fingers spread, and palms down. Slowly she moved them a little to one side, then a little to the other. Skang stared at her. Her face was shining as if it were sprinkled with drops of water. Her mouth was open and her cheeks were moving in and out.

"Fish, fish, I come into you," she whispered, her mouth shaping the words slackly in between small gasps, her hands moving more strongly, more surely.

"Fish, fish, I am in you, swimming. I am swimming and seeking, swimming and seeking, and I am finding, finding... "

Her hands ceased moving for a moment. "Water is good; it holds, it smoothes. Water is good. I seek through water. Here, here, here, here... " her voice bubbled as if there were phlegm in her throat. "Here, here, here, I am finding, finding, finding, finding, and I bite!"

At the last word her mouth snapped shut. Her hands stopped moving, and the line jerked. Skang pulled on it, and felt a throbbing, twisting, swerving weight that fought against the pull.

"Strong," he gasped, "strong."

Plara stood behind him and put her hands on his shoulders.

"Fish come!" she whispered, and the weight on the line no longer fought the pull. Skang dragged the fish up onto the ice and stared at it in wonder.

"It is big," he said.

Plara said nothing but turned away. He could not hear the words she spoke to the surrounding air, but he saw her lift her hands up to the sky and bring them back again to her breasts three times. When she turned back her face was placid. "In Her, Through Her," she said matter of factly. Then she looked directly into Skang's eyes and her eyes were as bright and cold as ice.

Skang felt a tightness in this throat.

"Ask!" said Plara.

Skang fumbled for words. "When I was a man of the Deer," he said slowly, "there was Bleng, the horned one, and Bleng called up the deer. You called up the fish." He bent over the fish, sliding the bone-hook round in the jaw till it was free of the sinewy lip.

"Can I call?" he asked.

Plara looked over his head at the trees, her eyes clouding. "It is the picture that came to me," she said, "There was a fish, and this is the fish. Look down into the hole in the stiff water, and tell what you see."

"I see my Other," said Skang.

"Look down through your Other."

Skang looked and the water was very dark, then smoky, and then he was no longer looking into the water but was standing in front of a great deer with many points. He walked up to the deer, which did not stir, and the deer spoke. It said, "Your breath is my breath," and a small white bird rose from between the antlers and flew up into the sky.

As Skang watched, the white bird became smaller and smaller until it was no longer a bird but a snowflake. There were tens and tens and tens of snowflakes coming down fast, and as they came closer they were all small white feathers, and, suddenly there was nothing but a black hole and dark water and his Other looking up at him.

He said aloud, "There was a deer and a white bird."

Plara laughed softly. "You have seen it?" she asked.

"Yes," Skang told her. "This is the one-feather in the wing," said Plara. "There will be a two-feather."

Skang felt dizzy. His stiff leg was aching.

"Pick up the fish," said Plara gently, "and put your finger in its mouth." Skang picked up the fish and put his finger in the open mouth. It was as if a cold snake ran up his arm from finger, to elbow, to shoulder, to neck, and into his head. He saw a wolf. It was white as the white bird and it was running between trees. He fitted an arrow to his bow, but the arrow slipped from his hands. He took another arrow. It would not fit the thong. He took a third arrow and it broke in his hand. He threw down the bow and the wolf stopped running. It stood very still and turned its head and looked at him. Its eyes were white as its fur and it gave a great leap into the air and fell. There were three arrows in its side. Skang stared at the red blood staining the white fur, and the redness became a bird and flew towards him. He held up his hand and caught it, and his hand was red and burning but there was no hurting in it. He stared at his burning hand and slowly opened the fingers. The bird had gone. He was standing again on the ice, his finger in the mouth of the fish.

"There was a white wolf and a red bird," he said.

"That is the two-feather," said Plara. She gazed into his eyes. "Hold the fish to your breast," she said softly.

Skang took his finger from the fish's mouth and held the fish to his breast.

"There is no picture," he said. "I see dark," and then he felt the fish grow heavy and heavier still and it writhed and jerked so that he could hardly hold it. It was the weight of a child, then of a woman, then of a strong not-woman.

"I cannot hold it," he cried.

"Hold it," came Plara's voice through the dark. "Hold it until the arms break."

He held it, and he felt the muscles tear, the bones pull apart, and the dark was no longer dark but the black mouth of a cavern that grew smaller and smaller until the blackness was a crow and the crow turned its yellow eyes towards him and there was nothing in his arms but the fish that lay against him wet and cold, as the crow faded like mist.

He gasped from the effort he had made. "Crow," he panted. "Cavern and crow."

"That is the three-feather," said Plara, "and you are Taken."

○

Chooser groaned. "It is ten darks to the full round of the moon," she muttered, "and there will be no Chooser."

Sweat shone from her brow. Manka, seated beside her in the dark hut, said nothing. Chooser twisted restlessly in her fur coverings. "You cannot take away the hurting?" she asked.

Manka sighed. "The reeds are knives," she said. "They cut my hands."

"This is in Her?" Chooser whimpered, "In Her, Through Her?"

Manka nodded. "All is in Her," she said. She closed her eyes and put her hands on the sick woman's brow.

"There is a binding upon your head," she said. "It is a binding of the Near-Taken." She paused.

"There are the Taken and they do not pleasure-choose and they hold the strong thinkings and happenings and the hidden happenings and thinkings and their bird-thinkings are of many colours and are swift. There are also the Near-Taken who stand at the pool and do not enter, who pick up the stone and mark it with spittle, who take what is given and do not give, and who choose. These are knives of the Near-Taken. I send out a bird-thinking and the bird does not come back. I put my hand to the reed mat and the reeds cut. There are rivers the deer cannot cross, and waterfalls the fish cannot leap."

"Then it is breath-ending?" asked Chooser.

"I can cut the thong," said Manka, "but all the choosings will spill out of you. You will have no ever-mind and your tongue will make no callings."

Chooser groaned once more. "The ever-mind is my breath," she said. Manka nodded. Chooser turned over on one side and stared at the dark walls of the hut. "There will be no Chooser for the Kindred," she said, "and a strong twig will be broken."

"There will be Change," said Manka, "but there will be Choosings."

"And a Chooser?"

Manka said sadly, "I have no thinking."

There was silence in the hut.

"Cut the thong," said Chooser. "I am Chooser no more."

○

Gron stared at the boar. It stood facing him, its huge shoulders flecked lightly with the falling snow, its eyes red, its tusks curved. It lowered its head and the mouth opened, a wet slit. Gron did not move. He could not. All strength had left. He stood as stiff as the bare tree beside him. Behind the boar there were rustling sounds, grunts, and shrill squeals. "Giftings," he told himself. He tried to put a picture of the fat giftings of the Kindred into his head but the picture moved like water and would not stay. He stared at the boar and suddenly it was not a boar but a deer with spread antlers, and red eyes, and then, in a breath, it was a boar again. He moved one finger and then another of the hand that held his spear. He breathed deeply. He summoned up the calling that is a wall against hurtings but the calling had no breath in it and the wall would not build. He stared into the red eyes and his own eyes burned, and his jaw loosened, and he heard himself snuffling, grunting. "It is my Other," he told himself confusedly. "It is my gifting-Other; it has my breath."

He put another picture in his head. It was a picture of the paces between them. Sweating, he stretched the paces out as a wet thong stretches. He watched the boar grow smaller, smaller, the red eyes still upon him. Stiff as a tree he stood, stretching out the snowy ground between them, and then, suddenly just as his hand upon the spear found strength to grip, the thong snapped and with a squeal the boar charged.

He pushed down on the spear and leapt upward, his muscles responding to the thrust as an arrow to the thong of the bow, and the boar passed under him, knocking the spear away, and crashed away through the snow-burdened bushes. He fell clumsily into the snow as the air filled with squeals and ten-and-ten giftings ran through the glade, some stumbling upon him. He raised himself to his feet, and looked down. The boar had torn aside the skins upon his leg and there was blood on his thigh. He pulled the skins aside. The red line was bright upon the skin, but there was no depth in it. His lungs took in great gasps of the chilled air. "In Her, Through Her," he muttered. "In Her, Through Her."

He lurched unsteadily against a younger tree and the shaken branches spilled their snow upon him as he slid into the dark.

○

"Chooser has a hurting," said Talker, "a strong hurting."

He smiled. Harn, binding a spear point to the shaft with tight thongs, grunted.

"There will be no Chooser at the full round of the moon," said Talker.

"A new Chooser will be called," said Harn. "It is the strong thinking. The Kindred will sit together and the ever-minded will tell the pictures in their heads and Caller will cry out at each picture 'Is it the Choosing?' and the Kindred will shout, and the big shout will make the Chooser."

Talker nodded. "The big shout," he said, "will be the shout of Harn and of the not-women. There will be no other shout as big."

Harn frowned. "The not-women will all see one picture?" he queried.

"I will tell you the picture," said Talker, "and you will tell the not-women. They will all be in one place at the Gathering and hold their spears before them."

"But Caller?"

"Fire-breath will be Caller at the Gathering," smiled Talker, "and Fire-breath will make one Calling."

"What woman will be called?" said Harn laying the spear aside.

Talker stood up and eased his cramped legs. "Her fire-breath will tell the Watchers," he said. He touched Harn lightly on the head. "In one moon or two, the not-women will pleasure-choose," he said, "and the women will be chosen and there will be Change."

Harn suddenly had a dryness in his throat. "It is a big twig to break," he muttered.

"It will be broken," said Talker.

○

102

Gron leaned on his spear and looked at the stiff water fringing the banks and the running darkness beyond it. "Tens and tens and tens of breaths," he told himself, "and tens and tens of paces."

The red line on his thigh stung like the sting of a briar, and there was a mist in his head. Through the mist he saw shapes drifting and changing: a deer and then a boar, a boar and then a fish, and then, suddenly, a running hare that leapt and scampered, leapt and scampered, its ears laid back, its scut flashing, its paws thudding on bare earth. He took a step and then another step. The cavern was close and sleep was near.

"A thin hurting," he told himself, "a thin hurting," but there was a throbbing in his thigh and a drumming in his head. He sent out a bird-thinking: *Plara, Plara.* The bird did not return. Step followed step, and breath breath. His shoulders hunched as under a great weight.

"It is the sleep," he told himself, "it is the great sleep that is breath-ending." He saw again the curve of the tusks and felt the line of fire upon his thigh. "So little a hurting, so deep a sleep," he murmured, for the mists were now two stones standing before him and he was in the stones, and, as he watched, they swayed like branches in the big wind.

"So deep a sleep," he repeated and then, the mist dividing before him, he saw the waterfall, the shouting water, its shouting stilled.

"Plara," he called and then, desperately, "Skang, Skang!"

He stood at the bottom of the curtain of stiff water and looked up and there was a black sun growing ever more black and the blackness filled his head and all the pictures were gone.

○

Chooser lay still under the heaped coverings. She closed her eyes. There was only blackness. She licked her dry lips and muttered, "Pictures come!" but no pictures came. Her arms and legs were heavy. She could move them only a little, and when she moved them the breath came quickly and the sweat started on her brow. "This is not waking and is not sleep," she told herself, "and it is not near-sleep. It is a log that lies in still waters and does not move. I am Log-Woman."

A shadow fell across her from the hut-opening as the skin curtain was pulled aside. It was Caller.

"The hurting has gone?"

"It has gone. Caller must make a new long-calling and a new short-calling. I am not Chooser. I am Log-Woman."

"That is not the calling," said Caller. She closed her eyes and put her hands to her head. "It does not come to me," she said, "but it will come."

Chooser closed her eyes again. "It is all black," she said. "It is all black."

○

Skang and Plara dragged Gron into the cavern. "It is a small scratch for a big sleep," said Skang, rubbing his stiff leg. Plara grunted. "Pull harder, Fish-Finder," she said. "You have had heavier burdens."

Together they laid their burden down and covered him with furs. Then Plara took shredded bark and the small clay pot and put the bark into the pot and, squatting over it, made yellow-water. She added leaves, and put it on the edge of the fire.

"It is a thin line," said Skang.

"It is thin as the knife moon," said Plara, "but it will grow full." She stirred the mixture in the pot.

"I have a thinking," said Skang suddenly and stood over Gron, his legs apart, letting the fur robe fall from him. Plara turned from the fire and watched as he lifted his hands up high then lowered them, all his fingers pointing at Gron, and "In the tines of the deer, the leap of the wolf, the gasp of the fish," he said, in a voice that echoed through the cavern, "the crow that falls is the crow that rises."

He swayed as he spoke. Plara sat back on her heels, her eyes wide. "This is the sleep," echoed Skang, "and this is the dream but sleep has ending, and the crow rides on the wolf." His hands fell to his sides. He was breathless and his face had lost all colour. He staggered and leaned against the wall of the cave. Plara, stirring the pot, said nothing.

Skang turned his head and looked at her.

"I am not Skang," he whispered. He slithered to his knees and, kneeling, looked at her.

"The Taken have near-sleep," said Plara gently, "and near-sleep is a moving water that finds deep pools."

Skang nodded. "I am Skang and sleep," he said and lay down on the floor of the cave, pulling the robe around him.

"Sleep," said Plara, taking the mixture in the bowl and pasting it upon a strip of hide.

"Sleep!" Skang grunted.

Gron, sweating under the pile of furs, moaned. Plara went to him.

○

Fleay rubbed the fat over her body carefully and slowly, enjoying the warmth of the rubbing, the slipperiness of her own skin.

"Fat of the giftings, warm, warm!" she muttered to herself, and "Through Her the cold, through Her the warm."

Her fingers lingered a little upon her breasts and she caressed the stiffening nipples. Then, with a sigh, she took more fat from the clay pot and rubbed her throat and shoulders. Her task finished, she pulled the robe around her, bound skins upon her legs and feet, and took up her spear. Talker, still half asleep, looked up from the pile of furs.

"You hunt?" he said in surprise, "There is no hunting in this cold."

Fleay said firmly, "I am ever-minded in this new light, and I hunt the picture that came into my head."

"Tell the picture," said Talker. He half sat up, leaning on one elbow.

Fleay shook her head. "If I give you the picture, Manka will take it from behind the reeds," she said, and she went out into the morning. Quickly she walked through the circle of huts, past the small fire where Fire-Maker was working, up to the place of the great fire where Grek was keeping the flames alight.

"In five darks the fire will be big," she told herself, "and there will be no Chooser and there will be Change."

She paused for a moment and looked at the opening in the wall and the picture came into her head again. It was of two not-women, and they were dragging something behind them through the snow. There were thongs around them and they were shouting, "In Her, Through Her! In Her, Through Her!" The thing they were dragging was made of fire-breath and the Kindred who suddenly were seated in the snow all about could not see the shape inside the fire-breath, but Fleay could see it; it was a woman with long black hair and as she looked at the picture the one not-woman was Talker and the two not-woman was Harn and the woman was the Other that had looked up at her from the dark pool. She held the picture in her head as she walked down the far side of the hill to the woodland. Once in the wood her pace slowed. The picture was changing. She looked at it, puzzled. The not-women were not Harn and Talker, and the woman was not Fleay.

105

She bit her lip. She struck her spear upon the earth and the picture was as it had been before. Now she was standing beside a pool. She looked at the stiff water and drove down with her spear again and again, making a big hole. Her Other looked up at her. She smiled at her Other.

"I am not bound," she said softly, "but you are bound. I am not Taken but you are Taken. I am in you but you are not in me." The dark water rippled. She stared into it. "Maker makes with Stone, Caller brings the Callings, Fire-Maker brings fire, Talker gives the thinkings, Chooser makes the Choosings," she said, "and these are the fish that the Kindred eat."

She pointed her spear at the water. "There is a great fish," she said, "that the Kindred have not seen. There is no picture of that fish in their heads, and it does not rise in the ever-mind or swim through near-sleep. It is the fish of Change that cannot be caught, but it comes to the net of one that is Taken and not-Taken. Come to the net!"

She stared into the waters. Warmth flowed up into her body from the feet, through the thighs and belly and breasts until her face flushed. The water was very still. She stared into it. Her eyes widened. She stood there a long time, staring.

○

Gron was crawling through the topmost branches of the trees. The sun was above him then below him, first on one side then on the other, and then it was in his head and it was burning, and he was in the sky rolling round and round and round. He watched himself spinning up above the trees. There was a bow in his hand. He fitted an arrow to the thong of the bow and sent it up at the spinning sun and then he was not the sun or the man watching the sun, but falling, falling, falling. His heart stopped. He had no breath. He was falling towards the trees. He tensed himself to meet the trees, but the trees flowed away from him like water. He readied himself for the shock of the earth but the earth too flowed away. He was falling through the earth, and he was stand-ing over a big hole in the earth watching himself falling. The hole was a dark pool. He lifted his spear and hurled it at the fish that was diving away from him. His heart began pounding. There was a gurgling in his throat and he was swimming up through the water, his lungs bursting. He dragged himself up over the edge of the pool, and looked up into a woman's face. It was the face of Plara. Her lips were moving. He heard the words. They were "Sleep, Sleep and Sleep In Her, Through Her." He sank to the earth. He was a stone and he was hot and he was wet and the air he breathed smelt of green leaves.

○

"It is the full round of the moon," said Talker, "and there is no Chooser." He stood between the two pillars, Harn beside him. "In the dark that is gone I stood in Her fire-breath and Her fire-breath came into me and I was in Her Womb." He glanced across the fire at Fleay. Her eyes glittered in the fire-glow and she was smiling. "In Her Womb there was a great water and it was dark. I looked into the water and the water opened as a mouth opens and I saw the gathering place and the fire and the Kindred. I saw Chooser. She stood here." He thumped the ground beside him with his staff. "I saw her go from here to the opening." He raised his staff and pointed at the opening in the enclosure behind the rows of seated Kindred. "She went out of the opening and there was no woman or not-woman in the track to stop her. It came to me than that none must leave the Gathering till the last calling is made, and none must come to the Gathering when the talk has begun, and that the Protector and strong not-women must be at that opening in every Gathering. That was the one-opening in the dark water."

He struck the earth once again with his staff, and the men moved to the opening and sat before it, their spears in their hands. Harn left Talker's side and went to them and stood there.

"This is not Chosen and is not Called," cried Bode with anger in her voice, and "Not Chosen, not Called," other voices echoed. Talker, alone now between the two tall stones, raised his voice.

"There is no Chooser to Choose, and what is not Chosen cannot be Called," he said, and then, hurriedly, "There was a two-opening of the dark waters."

"The one-opening was a wide opening," said Manka, quietly, "and the fish has come through the net." She looked across the fire at Talker and her eyes widened. There was a redness like fire around his head. She crossed her arms upon her breast. "In Her, Through Her, this Change," she muttered, "In Her, Through Her."

"The two-opening," said Talker loudly, "was the Talking and the Choosing and the Calling, and it was a picture of the black opening of the Womb. Fire-breath came from the opening and made a shape. The shape ran down the hill and among the Kindred and one said "Bush" and one said "Tree" and one said "Stone." Then a woman with the feathers of birds around her head and throat said "Spear," and a woman with the skull and the bones of Kraw made a loud hearing and the hearing was "Net," and the Kindred all shouted "Net." Then the fire-breath from Her womb became red and fire came down upon the Kindred and the one-woman and the two-woman were burned."

"Chooser and Caller," muttered Bode. "The women are Chooser and Caller," and "Chooser, Caller" other voices whispered.

"Her fire-breath is not for Choosing," said Talker. "It is a strong thinking and a loud hearing. That is the meat when the skin is taken."

"No Chooser, no Caller, but Talker alone?" said Bode, her face flushed, her hands clenched.

"That is not all the meat," said Talker, "Fire-breath is Fire-breath and is not Chosen; talk is talk and is Chosen and Called."

"Who will say fire-breath is fire-breath and talk talk?" said Fland, leaning forward on her haunches, "Who will put meat in the one-hand and in the two-hand?"

Talker said coldly, "There are three of the long-minded that are at the fire. It is not one, but one and one and one that breathe Her breath."

"It is not Chosen and Called," said Bode, stubbornly.

"It is Her breath," said Talker.

Two women rose to their feet. "This is not a Gathering," said one. They walked to the opening. Harn levelled his spear. They turned and went back.

"There was a three-opening of the dark waters," said Talker, "and it was my Other standing between two stones. My Other looked on the one side and the stone was woman and the stone had one face." He touched the stone with his staff. "My Other looked on the two side and it was not-woman and it had a one-face and a two-face." He touched the second stone. "And the two stones were the side-stones, the opening to her hut which is Her womb. And my Other looked into my eyes and the staff in my hand became the tree stone of the hut opening."

He lifted his staff and placed it across the two stones, and the fire between him and the Kindred sputtered and a dense cloud of smoke rose into the air. Fleay, in the front row of the Kindred, coughed. Tears came into her eyes. Manka, her eyes upon Fleay, smiled grimly.

"It is not fire-breath but water-breath," she told herself. She closed her eyes and through the dark she heard Talker calling out "Her fire-breath is here, is here, is here. We have made the opening to Her womb, and I breathe Her fire-breath. I breathe it. The Talker, the Chooser, the Caller are three as the one-stone and the two-stone and the staff are three, and the three are the opening to the Womb and the Womb is one and is Her."

There were beads of froth at the corners of his lips. He rocked backwards and forwards on his feet. "A picture comes to me," he shouted. "A picture comes, a picture comes, a picture comes. I am my Other. I am in the Opening of the Womb. I am Her breath. I am Long-Minded Breath-Giving Womb-Speaker. That is my Calling." He flung his arms out wide. "It is Her fire-breath that is Chooser," he shouted. "Is it the Choosing?" and there was a shout from the spear carriers at the opening, "It is the Choosing."

Talker raised both his hands, touching staff upon the stones. "The Gathering has ending," he said. "In Her womb we lie this dark, and in our bodies She keeps Her presence." Fleay chuckled.

○

Manka looked at the three brown pebbles in her hand. "Talker," she murmured, "Harn, Fleay." She held the three pebbles tightly then dropped them into the water bowl and bent over it. "Hers are the eyes; Hers is the calling; Hers is the hand," she murmured, and "Change is over all."

She looked for a long time. Outside the cavern the gently drifting snow grew thicker. A wind whispered and then whined. The snowflakes were smaller, hard. Manka held up her hands. "In Her, Through Her," she cried. She picked the bowl up in her hands and spilled it; the three dark pebbles rolled before her to the very lip of the cave, and on one of them was a speck of grey dust, and on another a speck of brown clay, and on the third a crack as thin as the hair of a woman and as black as the black of the wood when the fire has gone. She stared down at the pebbles and then, gathering her furs around her called, "O Mother, send! O Mother, send! O Mother, send!" rocking back and forward on her heels.

The pebbles lay still in front of her. The snowflakes were smaller still and sped past the cavern opening swift as the swiftest spears, and the wind howled as a wolf howls and the sky was black. "Send, O send!" cried Manka, "Send, O send!" and then, more quietly, the pain beneath her breasts sharpening, "In Her, Through Her this Change, this Change In Her, Through Her."

○

TEN

Plara stared out at the thickly falling snow, and, huddling her cloak around her, threw more wood on the fire. Skang rose from the bed of skins and limped to her side. "There is a picture in your head?"

She nodded. "It is a hurting," she said, "and there is fire in it."

Gron stirred uneasily in his sleep. "In ten darks he will be Crow-Thinker again," said Skang, "and the one and the two and the three will Wander."

Plara stared at him curiously. "That is from near-sleep?"

Skang nodded. "It comes to me that Crow-Thinker and Wolf-Runner and White Bird go to the people of the Unk, to the Kindred, and there are hurtings and breath-endings."

"And there is fire," added Plara. She shuddered.

"Eat and sleep," said Skang. "In sleep there are thinkings."

Plara turned away from the fire and they went back to the bed of skins and furs, and lay down beside Gron. Plara sat up suddenly, her eyes wide. "There is a three-stone," she said, "there is a three-stone."

"Sleep," said Skang. Plara slept.

○

Talker, leaning on his staff between the two pillars of stones, surveyed the huddled fur-swathed Kindred. "It comes to me in the fire-breath," he said, his voice gentle and slow. "I see one walking into the Womb. It is one who has passed through breath-ending." He stared into the fire. "It comes to me," he said, "the walk is slow for there is no breath in the body." He lifted his voice. "I have a strong thinking that the Kindred that find breath-ending be set upon their feet and be given fire-breath to walk tall into the Womb. I am Her fire-breath and I choose that a big stone high as a not-woman be put by the Body-Fire, that the body be thonged to the stone, and that fire be put about it. The Kindred will go strong into the Womb with the breath that is Hers. Is it Chosen?" The men gathered at the opening to the Burning Place lifted their spears and spoke with one voice: "It is Chosen."

"Then let it be a Calling and a loud hearing," cried Talker, and Caller, seated before him, her face red in the glow from the fire raised her voice that had a huskiness in it and said, "A big stone will be put at the place of burning and those that find breath-ending will be thonged to the stone and fire will burn them."

She coughed, her body shaking. Talker looked across the fire at Harn, standing with the spear carriers.

"Strong not-women will carry the stone," he said, "and Maker will put marks upon it." Maker, seated between Caller and Fire-Maker, muttered, "In Her, Through Her." Fleay on the other side of the fire stared at Caller, her eyes narrow, her mouth a straight line. Caller bent forward, coughing.

○

There is one finger of snow," said Gron, gathering up arrows. "We will see the marks of the hare."

Skang nodded. "I come," he said.

Together they half clambered, half slid down the icy rocks past the frozen curtain of the waterfall and made their way into the trees. The air was still. There was no wind. The boughs above them creaked with snow and from time to time a flurry of white would fall. Skang hissed and pointed with his bow. There was one track and then two. They followed the tracks, then Gron took Skang's arm and held him still. The tracks led to a huge tree with a gaping hole at its base. They squatted down in the snow, two humps of brown fur, their bows drawn. "Come," said Gron inside his head, "White leaper, white leaper, fat white leaper come!" He made a picture of grass in his head and of sweet leaves. He breathed in the chill air and gave it the smell of grass and blew the smell towards the tree. A branch above him twitched and a handful of snow fell. He did not move. The air was chill, the sun pale. "Come, come," whispered Gron inside his head, and then drew in his breath sharply as a hare peered out of the darkness of the hollow tree and then quickly withdrew.

Skang said in his head, "Wind be still, air be still, arrow be quick to end breath." The white head with its shining brown eyes appeared again, and the hare lolloped out onto the snow. Two arrows flew as one, and the hare gave a wild squeal, knocked backwards into the tree.

Skang grunted with satisfaction and got to his feet, and the two of them went up to the tree. The hare gleamed white in the dark of the riven trunk. Gron went in. He said, "It is fat."

His words echoed. He stood up inside the tree, holding the hare by its long back legs.

"Fat," he said again, listening to the echo. "There are two hearings," he said, "a big and a small hearing."

Again the words echoed. Skang came into the tree and stood beside him. "It is a long-minded tree," he said. "It has many tens and tens of moons in it."

"It makes hearings," said Gron thoughtfully. He reached upwards and rapped his bow against one side of the darkness and then another.

"There is a one-sound and a two-sound," he said. He rapped again in another place. "And a three-sound."

"Pebbles in an empty pot," said Skang, moving out of the tree. Gron followed him slowly. He looked around him. A bough of the tree had fallen and lay three paces away. It was as thick as his thigh and hollow and the fall had broken it so that one piece was no longer than his arm from finger to elbow. He hit it on one end with his bow, and then he hit it in the middle. Skang picked it up and put it on his shoulder. "It will burn," he said.

Gron looked at him. "It will make Callings," he said.

○

Manka squatted down beside Caller in the dark hut. Snow had begun to fall again. "There is a fire-worm in my neck," whispered Caller, "and there are fire-worms in my breath. I can make no loud hearing. Is it breath-ending?" Suddenly contorted, she coughed and choked.

"There is blood in my mouth," she panted, and spat.

Manka put the small clay pot to the bloodied mouth and murmured, "Drink!"

Caller drank. "When I am in the Womb there will be no Caller," she gasped, "and the Kindred . . . . . " She coughed again, deep coughs that wrenched her.

Manka said gently, "Breath-ending is birth-beginning."

Caller shuddered. "Is it one dark or two?" she asked.

Manka did not answer. She stood up and held her hands out, palm downwards, over the restless body. "Sleep," she said, "sleep, In Her, Through Her."

The woman's eyes closed. A small cough racked her momentarily. A little bubble of red burst at the corner of her mouth. Manka stood still as stone, feeling that warmth rise up through her body and flow down her arms to her fingers. She pressed her hand downwards as if the air was a solid thing, then turned and left the hut. The snow was falling more thickly, and the wind was rising.

○

Plara sat cross-legged in front of the hollow log. She hit it with a stick, first in one place then another. "The big end makes a big hearing like a not-woman," she said, "and the small end makes a woman-hearing." She turned the log on end and hit it again. "It is a bigger hearing." She turned to Gron. "It comes to me to put a skin on it," she said, "and the skin will make the hearing big. It will be an empty pot with a skin on it."

Gron brought a scraped deer skin and thonged it tight around the end of the log and Plara laid the log on its side again and hit it with the stick. The sound was louder. She turned it on end again and hit the taut skin. The sound was louder still. "It has one- and two-callings," she said, "and the skin has a three-calling." She tapped the skin in three places. "There are many callings," she said, her eyes wide, "Bring a two-skin."

Gron brought it and stretched it over the other end of the log and thonged it tight. Plara laid the log over her crossed knees and hit it with a stick, first on one skin and then on the other, and then on the body of the log.

114

"It is a bird-calling," she whispered. "It is a woman and a not-woman and a bird-calling."

"And a hare thumping," said Gron, "and the calling of stone on stone" and then, reaching over, he slapped one skin with the flat of his hand. "And the breaking of stiff water," he added.

Skang said suddenly, "There are two hands to hit," and gave Plara another stick. She bent over the log, absorbed, her eyes narrow, her brow furrowed.

"Quick. Quick," urged Skang. Quickly she struck the skins, the wood, the skins again and Skang stood up.

"It is running," he said and he moved his feet up and down and then a little forward and a little back. Plara struck more slowly.

"It is walking," said Gron, jumping to his feet. Plara giggled. She struck as quickly as she could, first on the skins then on the wood, over and over again.

"It is jumping," shouted Skang and he leapt up. Gron did the same. Plara suddenly excited, shouted out. "Hill-Builder, Womb-Filler, Reed-Breaker, Fire-Breather, Tree-Shaper, Fish-Swimmer, Deer-Caller, Change-Maker, Breath-Singer, Bird-Hurler, Wolf-Runner, Great Gatherer, dance in me the Dance."

She opened her eyes wide. She said, in wonder, "It is Dance. It comes to me that this is Dance, and it is Dance-Maker that has come to the Womb."

Gron stood stock-still, his eyes bright. "It is loin-stirrer," he said.

Plara held the log to her breasts. "It is blood-bringer," she said in a low voice. "It comes to me that it is Blood-Bringer, Loin-Stirrer, Dance-Maker and the short-calling that comes to me is Dom. Dom," she repeated, striking the taut skin with the flat of her hand. "Dom," she said, "Dom. It is Dom." The three of them stared at the log and then at each other. "It is Dom," they said.

○

"Is it a straight path?" Manka asked, squatting beside Caller.

"It is a straight path," came the answering whisper so low that Manka had to lean forward to hear it.

"Are the happenings heavy?"

"Some are light and some are heavy."

"Give me the heavy happenings that I may bear them for you."

The slack lips moved, but no sound came from them. Manka leaned closer. A sudden pain struck below her breast. She drew in her breath sharply.

"Speak," she commanded, "Speak."

Caller ran her tongue over her dry lips. Her voice was half a whisper, half a rattle. "I made callings that were not In Her, Through Her. I made a new long-calling for Flower-Lipped Herb-Gatherer and it was Big-Eating Fur-Hole. We bed-shared the one dark and the two dark she pleasure-chose, and there was a hurting in me."

"This I will carry."

Caller sighed. The sigh bubbled in her throat. "Ten moons gone Chooser gave me Small-Eared Bone-Sharpener to put the callings into her head. I did not put them into her head. There is no Caller to sit on my stone at the gathering. This is a heavy happening."

"I will carry."

The voice grew fainter still. "There are more."

Manka held her hands out over the troubled face. "Speak," she whispered, "Speak!"

"I cannot speak. My feet are on the path."

"I carry all the happenings," murmured Manka. "In Her, Through Her. All Things, All Ways." She gazed into the mist that formed before her eyes and there again was the track up the hill and the figure of a woman walking towards the cavern. She began to follow. The hill was steep. She put one foot forward and then another. The weight upon her shoulders almost bent her double. The pain under her breast grew sharper. Her arm throbbed. The cavern was a long way ahead. Slowly she followed the figure. At the mouth of the cave, stumbling, breathless, she paused for a moment and then, with a deep breath, stood straight. "It is given and it is taken," she said. Then, as the cave melted away, a blackness came into her head and she fell forward upon the woman whose breath had ended a moment before.

○

Skang and Gron leaned on their spears at the edge of the clearing. The snow before them lay smooth and unbroken. Skang sniffed the air. "The deer have gone," he said. Gron knelt down and scrabbled in the snow, baring a tuft of grass. He dug into the earth around the grass with his stone knife and pulled it up. He put his hand upon the bared earth and closed his eyes. "Paeg," he said. He stood up and thrust the point of his spear into the brown earth so that the spear stood up in front of him. He looked at the spear. The spear did not move. He walked round it slowly, his fur-clad feet making big prints in the snow. He looked at the spear again. It had begun to lean to one side. He pulled it out of the ground and pointed it in the direction it had leaned. "Paeg," he said again, and set off across the broad expanse of snow, Skang following.

○

It took four men to carry the long stone up the hill to the burning place, and they stopped many times on the journey. They lay it down on its side a little way from the fire which was smouldering dully, and began to dig a hole with their stone knives. The earth was hard. Maker stood to one side and watched them. He had made marks on the stone, biting them into it with a fury he did not understand. The marks had come to him as he made them. He stared at them once again, the one-mark, the two-mark, and the three-mark. His hands ached. He thrust them deeper inside his furs. The hole was deep enough and the four men stood over the stone, stretching their arms and loosening the bunched muscles of their shoulders.

"It is a big pleasure-thing," said one of them, grinning.

"And the fur-hole is deep," said the second.

They laughed. "Earth-Woman pleasure-chooses," said the first one, and together the four lifted the stone, and, staggering, brought its base to the lip of the hole.

Maker turned away. His throat was dry and his heart was pounding. "In Her, Through Her," he muttered, but the words rattled emptily in his head. He heard the four men grunt and then a thump as the stone plunged into the hole. The earth shook. He turned back with an effort and watched the men packing the earth tight around the stone.

"Caller chooses a big not-woman," said the first man. "She will not bed-share this dark."

The other three laughed. Bile rose up in Maker's throat. Underneath his furs his hands gripped each other. The smallest of the three men said, "What are the marks calling?" Maker cleared his throat. "The marks are In Her, Through Her," he said. "I have no thinking." He stared at them again. "It comes to me . . . ," he said, and then stopped, biting his lip. He walked away from the stone, and out of the Burning Place and down the hill, and his head was filled with a picture of fire, and in the fire a bird.

○

The dead pig swung side to side on the pole the men bore between them shoulder to shoulder as they walked in single file along the bank of the frozen river. At every second or third step a bright drop of blood fell upon the white snow. They were in sight of the frozen waterfall when Skang, who was leading, stopped. "There is a Calling," he said. Gron lifted his head. Through the still air came a low sound like far thunder and then a sound like the patter of rain upon leaves.

"It is Dom," said Gron. "Dom is hurting." They stood still for a moment and then the sound changed. It was the hooves of many deer upon hard earth.

"It is running," said Skang, and broke into a trot. The sound grew quicker, frantic.

"It is hurting and running," gasped Gron and together they dropped their burden in the snow and ran. As they clambered up to the ice curtain the sound grew sharper, clearer. They stumbled into the cavern. Plara was standing before the fire. She had slung Dom round her neck with a broad thong, and was beating it with the two sticks. Her eyes were wide and frightened, and she was leaning back on her heels, her legs apart, panting. On seeing the two men she let her hands fall to her sides.

"It has come to me. The Calling has come to me. In near-sleep it has come. The fire broke as a stone breaks and in it there was dark. I went into the dark and stood in the place of the Kindred. I made a loud hearing to Chooser and Chooser came out of her hut. Her eyes and her mouth were black as burned sticks and she said, 'I am Log-Woman.' I turned and made a loud hearing to Caller and Caller came out of her hut. Her body was bare and fire was on her body. She said, 'I have found breath-ending.' Then she was all fire and when the fire was gone there was a pile of burned bones. I turned to the track up the hill and sent a bird-thinking to Manka. Manka came out of the cave. There was a great spear in her body below her breasts. I ran towards her, and as I ran she fell forward into the snow and three birds flew out of her, a white bird and a black bird and a red bird and they flew to me and there was a sound like the breaking of a great stone and my head was filled with dark and I was in the Womb with Dom and I was here, and I took up Dom . . . . . "

She swayed on her feet. Gron leapt forward and held her, his arm around her shoulders. She breathed hard for a moment and then freed herself from his grasp.

"We go to the Kindred," she said.

"It is the deep cold," said Gron, "We go when the stiff water runs again."

Plara shook her head. "We go," she said, "We go."

○

Fleay looked at her hands, spreading the fingers wide. She made fists of them, digging the nails into her palm, and then stretched the fingers again holding them stiff as twigs. She felt heat flowing into her hands down from her shoulders. The woman lying on the pile of skins groaned, and pressed her swollen belly.

"Manka," she whispered, "Manka."

"Manka is in her cave," said Fleay briskly, "She is not of the Kindred."

The woman arched her back and lifted her knees. "It comes," she gasped, "It comes."

Fleay knelt between the legs and put her hands on the belly. "Womb open, birth come!" she whispered. "Fish come to my hand," and she cupped her hands between the woman's legs. The woman groaned again. Her head threshed from side to side. Fleay's fingers were stiff. They were filled with heat. They were pointed as spears. No, not spears. They were hooks to pull out the fish. No, not hooks.

She whispered, "Hear me! Hear me! Come! Come!"

She pushed the woman's thighs apart. The woman threw her head back, her eyes squeezed shut.

"Come! Come!" shouted Fleay. "Fish through the net. The net is open. Fish, Fish, through, through!" Her hands were suddenly fists. The woman gave a great heave and a shout and the flesh stretched and round, red, and wet, a head thrust out of her and quick as a fish the child slid onto the skins.

"Breath begins," shouted Fleay in triumph, but breath had not begun. The little wet body lay still upon the fur. Frantically Fleay lifted it by its slippery heels and slapped once, again, then again.

The woman opened her eyes. "Woman?" she asked, "or not-woman?"

Fleay stood up. A great rage filled her head. "Not-birth," she said harshly, "It is not-birth."

She laid the child down on the skins at the woman's feet. She did not wait for the rest of it, but went out of the hut. Talker, leaning on his staff a few paces away, looked into her face.

"Not-birth," said Fleay briefly, "Burn it."

Talker nodded. Fleay looked back at the hut she had left. "Send a woman," she commanded, and walked from the circle of huts. At the edge of the forest she looked at her hands. They were red. "Spears and hooks," she told herself, "spears and hooks," and then, to her own astonishment, her breast heaved and her eyes filled with tears.

○

The short winter day was almost over before Plara, Skang and Gron reached the place where the waterfall began. Wordlessly they dragged their fur-wrapped bundles across the snow to the edge of the forest. Plara knelt down and opened one bundle and took out the fire-stick. She squatted in the snow. Gron and Skang, knives in hand, went into the forest and broke dry wood from the under-bellies of bushes and snapped off lower branches from the trees. Skang bit his lip. "Wolf?" he said, raising his head, sniffing the air.

"Plara will make a wall of spears and fire and hurting," said Gron. "Wolf will not come."

Skang shuddered. "Wolf will come," he said in a low voice. "This is the dark that Wolf will come."

They carried the dry wood back to Plara, and she made fire. Seated cross-legged around the fire, they stared at the frozen river.

"Wolf comes on stiff water," said Skang. "It is the Great Wolf."

Plara threw more dry wood on the fire. "Sleep," she said, "Sleep In Her," and pulling her furs over her head she curled up on the snow. Gron did likewise. Skang rested his spear beside him and lay back, staring up at the clear sky, and the moon that was almost full.

"How many darks to the Kindred?" he asked.

"Ten and ten and ten," said Gron. "In two darks it is the full round of

120

the moon and then in ten and four darks it is the dark of the dark and we come to the Kindred."

He closed his eyes. Plara was already sleeping.

"The people of the Unk," Skang murmured, and himself drifted towards sleep, only to sit up, the hairs upon his nape as sharp as sharp grass. He stared out over the river; there was a shape moving on the farther bank. Slowly, cautiously, he rolled onto his hands and knees, his spear in his hand. Inch by inch he moved away from the fire to the river, and crouched on the shore. He breathed in the smell of the fire and the smell of the furs about him, and he breathed out the smell of deer. He put a young deer in his head; his arms were the front legs of the deer and his legs were the back legs and his head had small horns upon it and his muzzle was wet. He stared across the ice that glinted in the shine of the moon and the shape he was watching moved onto the ice. It was a single wolf, pale in the moonlight. He crouched lower, putting his spear beneath him, the butt between his legs, the shaft gripped in two hands, one in front of the other, and the blade pointing at the wolf that moved closer. Behind him, twenty paces away, Gron and Plara did not move in their furs and the fire flickered gently. Slowly the wolf approached, its paws careful on the ice. It paused and raised its head. "It is the Great Wolf," Skang told himself. His heart thudded. He saw in his head the white wolf of his Taking, the three arrows, the blood on the white fur, and the red bird. The wolf pawed the ice. It sniffed at the still air. In Skang's head the arrows murmured softly. "Gron, Plara, Skang," they murmured, "Three for the Great Wolf and Skang is the bow."

There was not a sound in the trees, not a rustle or shudder of leaf. Skang took a slow deep breath. "Come," he whispered. The wolf came. It was ten paces away, then eight, then five. Skang was a young deer. He was a deer lost. He made the sound the wolf knew. The wolf covered the last five paces in a leap and Skang thrust upward with the spear and it was through the wolf's throat and the wolf, all four paws scrabbling and skidding on the ice, twisted and turned; the black jaws opened and a cry rang out over the stillness, and it fell, legs twitching, eyes dulled pebbles, blood dark upon the whiteness. Skang stood. His legs trembled. He looked back at the fire. Gron and Plara were also standing. "Wolf," he said, "Wolf." He took hold of the hind legs of the wolf and dragged it towards the fire. "It is the white wolf," he said, and

121

then, "Make Dance," he cried, "Make Dance," and Plara took up Dom and two sticks and the sticks beat slow and then fast and faster still and Skang and Gron and Plara herself, feet stamping, to the thumps and clicks and shudders of the sound, went round and round the fire, and "It is the Dance," cried Plara to the riding moon, "In Skang the Dance, in Skang the Dance!"

O

ELEVEN

Manka sat at the opening of her cave, the fire behind her flickering redly. Her head was bowed and half hidden under its fur hood. Bode, Freng, and Polla, squatted before her. "There is no Chooser," said Bode, "and there is no Caller."

Manka said nothing. The pain beneath her breasts was sharp; her breath came with difficulty.

"Protector stands with the not-women and they bring spears to the gathering and make a loud hearing at the Choosing," said Freng.

"Fire-Maker is a broken twig," added Polla, "and there is a thinking that Manka is not of the Kindred."

They gazed into Manka's face. Manka was silent.

"It comes to me," said Bode, "that Talker is Chooser and Caller, that Protector is a spear in his hand, Fire-Maker the skins under his feet, and Maker the bowl for his drink."

"It is Change," said Manka, "It is Change, and Change is In Her."

Bode flushed. She said angrily. "Manka was in her cave when Shalla had birth-beginnings. Talker sent Fleay to her, and it was a not-birth. Was it Fleay who changed that breath-beginning to breath-ending?"

"I have no thinking," said Manka. She lifted her head and gazed out over the snow to the Burning Place on the hill beyond the giftings.

Bode said, "This dark there is a burning. Caller will burn and will hold the not-birth to her breasts, and Talker will be Chooser and Caller and he will make strong thinkings. She leaned forward. "O Fire-Handed Breath-Changer," she said, using the long-calling, "Bode that is Three-Birth Reed-Twister, Freng that is Big-Breasted Skin-Scraper, Polla that is Long-Armed Fish-Finder, have hurtings in their heads. Take out the hurtings."

Manka spoke slowly. "When water runs fast and deep it will not stop at a mat of reeds. I have been in near-sleep and I have been ever-minded and it has come to me that there is one Chooser and it is Her. There are pictures in my head. There are three women with spears and they throw the spears. The spears turn round in the air and the women throw up their hands and the spears bring the breath-ending. This is a picture the wind must blow away."

Freng said carefully, "A woman pleasure-chooses Harn. There is a knife in her hand that dark and Harn finds breath-ending."

Manka frowned. "Kindred do not bring breath-ending to Kindred. That knife is the big wolf in the pack. The pack will follow and tear down tens and tens of deer."

"A picture of the Kindred comes into my head," said Polla, "and the Kindred are all women and little ones." She spat into the snow.

"Woman and not-woman came from Her womb," said Manka, "and if the not-women are gone the womb will wither and break and the Kindred will find breath-ending but no breath-beginning."

The three women sat silent, staring at her. Manka threw back the hood of her cloak and looked up into the grey sky. "It is a hidden thinking that comes to me," she said. "A woman finds breath-ending and is burned, but her womb brings birth to one and two and three. The one is Wolf. The two is Kraw. The three is a white bird. There is a knife that is not of stone or bone. There is a spear that flies. There is a tree that walks and runs and leaps." She lowered her head and looked into Bode's eyes. "When the deer run to the hunter," she said, "the hunter waits."

"We will wait," said Bode.

○

"I choose the beginning," cried Talker, standing tall between the two stones. "She is with us, within us, around us, and we are together in Her."

He looked across the fire at the rows of the Kindred, and then pointed his staff at the stone pillar set up a little way apart from the fire. Caller's naked body, thonged to the stone, shone red in the flames. The thong over her forehead held her head high. In between her breasts the stillborn child faced the gathering, its small fists clutched tight, its eyes sealed shut. Dry branches and twigs were piled at the foot of the pillar.

"It is the full round of the moon," cried Talker, "In Her, Through Her, this full round of the moon."

He crossed his arms upon his chest. "Breath is taken," he chanted, and then, his arms flung wide, "Breath is given." His voice rose. "It is the hour of Callings. I make the Callings."

Fleay, seated in the front row of the Kindred, leaned forward expectantly. She rehearsed the new long-callings in her head. Bode would be new-called Fat-Breasted Reed-Plucker, Freng, Loud-Breathing Slow-Walker. She giggled to herself. Fire-Maker would be long-called Small-Eyed Earth-Croucher. Her own long-calling she had whispered to herself many times. "Quick-Fingered Breath-Helper."

She looked over her shoulder to see if Manka were among the Gathering. Manka would have no long-calling. She was not of the Kindred. The Callings continued. Some of the Kindred were restless. The women were muttering. The children looked frightened. A baby cried. Talker lifted his voice still higher as he came to his own long-calling.

"Long-Minded, Snow-Headed Talker is new-called Strong-Choosing, Loud-Calling, Fire-Breath," he chanted and then, rapidly, "Is it chosen?"

"It is chosen" came the shout from the spear carriers. The women on either side of Manka looked at her. She murmured gently, "You may call a fish a bird but it will not fly."

"There was no long-calling for Manka," said one of the women loudly from the middle of the Gathering.

Talker said levelly, "Manka is not of the Kindred."

"Then she is Outer-Thing?" asked Polla, astonishment in her voice.

Talker raised his staff to quell the babble. "She is Outer-Thing and she is not Outer-Thing," he said, "She is of the Cavern and not of the Kindred."

"Then I am of the Cavern," shouted Bode.

"And I," "And I," "And I," echoed other women's voices.

Manka rose to her feet. All looked at her. She threw back the hood of her furs and it seemed, as she lifted up her arms, that she was taller than the tallest in that place. She said, "Manka alone is of the Cavern. No one of the Kindred may come into it, for the Cavern is not of the Kindred. It is of Her, in Her, through Her. Before the next full round of the moon there will be no Manka. She returns to the Womb to find breath-beginning. Manka goes but the Cavern will not go. The Cavern is of Her. It is Her Womb."

Talker lifted his staff. "There is a strong thinking ... ," he began.

Manka passed one hand across her mouth. Talker fell silent.

"The foot of Manka is on the path," she said, "Her back bends under the heavy happenings, and she climbs the path alone. She will stand at the mouth of the Womb and the Womb will open."

She crossed her arms upon her breast, then very slowly spread them wide, lifting her hands to the sky. "Breath is taken, Breath is given," she said and then, letting her hands fall to her sides she almost whispered, "There is Change. Change is In Her Through Her."

She turned on her heel and walked to the opening. The spear carriers hesitated. Harn spoke first. "There is a strong thinking that the Kindred cannot go from the Gathering," he said and he pointed the blade of his spear towards her.

Manka looked at him. "That spear is broken," she said. She made a fist of her hand, and Harn, clutching suddenly at his belly, doubled over, grunting with pain.

"I go," said Manka, gently. "The tree must bend to the wind" and she went through the opening.

Talker, his hand clutched to his speechless throat, watched her from between the big stones. At last his voice returned.

"Outer-Thing," he screeched, "Outer-Thing! The long-calling and the short-calling is Outer-Thing. Is it Chosen?"

"It is not Chosen," called Bode, "It is not Chosen."

Harn, once again upon his feet, gestured to the spear carriers, his face flushed with rage. "It is Chosen," he shouted, and the spear carriers echoed him. "It is Chosen," he shouted, and the spear carriers echoed him. "It is Chosen! It is Chosen!"

There was a shocked silence. Fleay leaned forward, her eyes red in the firelight. "Manka is Outer-Thing and Not Outer-Thing," she said, "She is not of the Kindred but of the Cavern. That is the Choosing."

She stared up at Talker. He gulped.

126

"The long-calling and the short-calling is 'Outer-Thing and Not Outer-Thing'" he said, "Manka is not of the Kindred. Is it Chosen?"

There was an indeterminate mumble of "Chosen" and "Not-Chosen."

"It is Chosen," said Talker firmly, and then, hurriedly, sweat standing out upon his brow, "Is there talk?"

"You are Talker," said Bode, sardonically. "There will be talk."

Talker struck the ground three times with his staff. "This dark there is a great burning," he said, "a two-burning, and the fire-breath will be strong. It has come to me in near-sleep and from the ever-mind that in this fire-breath there will be Change and strong thinkings. I have a picture in my head; it is of the new knife moon, and the filling moon, and the full round of the moon and the women are pleasure-choosing. Woman is one from the Womb, but there is a two from the Womb and it is not-woman. I see the full round of the moon, and the emptying moon, and the moon-ending and then there is no moon, and She is not above us, and the not-women are pleasure-choosing."

There was a quick gasp from among the Kindred.

"It is Through Her that it comes to me. In the dark of the dark when there is no moon the not-women choose and the women are chosen."

"This is the strong thinking fire-breath will bring?" asked Polla, "The burning has not begun. You have a picture of what it will bring?"

Talker lifted his staff. "It is Change," he said, "The watchers will not be three but all the Kindred. Make the fire!"

Fire-Maker took up a long stick with a bundle of twigs thonged to it. She thrust the twigs into the fire and then, as they crackled and blazed, she pushed them into the wood at the base of the pillar upon which Caller and the stillborn child hung. In a moment the fire was blazing. The Kindred gaped, the children screamed, the fire leapt upwards. There was a rich heavy smell. The hair on Caller's head sputtered and flamed, then suddenly out of her mouth came a tongue of flame, green and orange and yellow, and out of the baby's mouth a flicker of blue, and Talker lifted his staff and cried, "It is Her fire-breath; it is the Change and the strong thinking. Is it Chosen?"

The Kindred sat silent, and then from Harn came the cry, "It is Chosen" and from the spear-carriers the same cry.

"Is it Chosen?" shouted Talker again, and the response was loud.

"It is Chosen."

A third time Talker struck the ground with his staff and a third time he called.

"It is Chosen," came the roar.

The thongs burned through and Caller and the child, now fully aflame, slid down the pillar. As they struck the burning boughs a shower of sparks flew up into the air and over the Kindred.

"The talk is over for this dark," cried Talker and then, lifting his staff high over his head, "In Her womb we lie this dark, and in our bodies She keeps Her presence."

The Kindred rose to their feet. They straggled out of the opening and down the hill to the hut fire. There was little talk. Harn and Talker were the last to leave. Fleay walked between them. She was smiling.

"Who will choose Fleay in the dark of the dark?" she wondered aloud. "Will one not-woman choose her, or two, or three, or ten?" She giggled. She rubbed gently against Harn. "Harn," she said softly, "I choose you this dark." Talker stood still. He gaped. Fleay laughed. "And I choose Talker. It is Change," she told him, "It is Change."

○

"Moon-ending is near," said Gron, staring up through the intertwined blackness of the trees. Skang, lying on the other side of Plara, huddled deeper into the furs and grunted. "It comes to me," said Gron, "that in the dark of the dark we will find the Kindred."

"We will go to the cavern of Manka," said Plara and then stopped.

"There is no Manka in my head," she whispered, clutching Gron's arm. "There is no Manka in my head. The cavern is an empty pot. There is dust in it and three pebbles. There is no Manka."

"There is Gron and there is Skang," murmured Skang to comfort her.

Plara stared up at the pale wisp of the moon, her eyes blurred with tears.

"There is Wolf and Kraw," Gron told her. She nodded in the darkness. A film of ragged cloud drifted across the dying moon.

○

Fleay left Harn and Talker sleeping. The snow outside the hut was still only a finger deep but the sky was grey. She squatted by the fire in between the huts and stared into it. She said to herself, in a soft whisper, "Quick-Fingered Breath-Helper," and looked down at her fingers, flexing them. She stretched them out and held them to the fire. She said, "Two-Choosing Quick-Fingered Breath-Helper" and smiled. "The one is Talker, who is long-minded and brings the Choosings, the Callings, and the strong thinkings," she told herself, and then, "The two is Harn who is Thick-Armed Spear-Hurler and brings the loud hearings to the Callings and Choosings and holds the not-women in his hand as a net holds fish." She wriggled her toes in their fur wrappings. "And the three is Fleay," she whispered, her eyes bright, "and the three is the thong round Talker and Harn." She giggled. "This coming dark is the dark of the dark," she told herself, "and the not-women will choose. Talker will choose Fleay."

She pushed a stray twig into the fire. There was a small spurt of flame.

"Harn," she told herself, "will choose Fleay."

She rose to her feet and turned back to the hut. At the entrance she paused. There was a stiffness in her legs, and her head was filled with a picture of Manka. She bent to pull the skins aside and go into the hut but there was a sudden pain in her back. She straightened up and turned. Mist filled her eyes. She found she was walking away from the huts and towards the cavern. She stopped and planted her feet firmly in the snow, but it was no use. She was a brown leaf in the wind, and the wind was carrying her up the hill. She tried to cry out, but could make no sound. Stumbling, she went up the hill to the cavern, her mouth slack-lipped and open, her breath whistling in her throat, her hands helpless at her sides.

○

Manka stepped out of the cavern and looked down at the young woman kneeling in the snow. Her black fur cloak glistened in the grey morning light. Her face was half hidden beneath her hood.

"Stand," she said.

Fleay stood. Manka, on the ledge of rock at the cavern's entrance, towered over her. Behind her the fire flickered and smoke drifted lazily out of the mouth of the cave.

"You are the Taken and Not-Taken," said Manka, "and you are a hurting in the Kindred. Your ever-mind is a red bird; your hand is a claw and your tongue is a knife."

She swayed a little on her feet. The pain beneath her breasts was sharper than ever and her arms were leaden. Fleay lifted her head. She spoke with an effort.

"You are Outer-Thing and Not Outer-Thing," she said, "You are not of the Kindred."

Manka said, very gently, "The tree is not of the leaves, the earth is not of the grass, the sky is not of the clouds; I am Of Her, In Her, Through Her; I am Manka and Not-Manka; I am woman and not-woman; I am of the Womb."

Fleay stared into the shadowed face. "There is a hurting in you," she said. "It is a big hurting. It is breath-ending." She tilted her chin upwards. Her eyes narrowed. "I send a spear," she hissed, "I send a spear through Manka." She pointed a finger. "I send a spear," she spat.

Manka did not move.

"I send fire," said Fleay, her voice more shrill, flickering the fingers of her hands like flames, "I send fire. I send fire."

Manka said nothing. Fleay, sweat pouring from her, lifted her hands above her head and moved them rapidly.

"I send waters to drown, waters to drown, waters to drown," she chanted.

Manka threw the hood back from her face. "The spear is broken, the fire is ash, the pool is emptied," she said. She held her hands out towards Fleay and Fleay stepped backwards one pace, then two, then three. It was as if a great wind were thrusting her away from the cavern. She braced herself against it, but then she felt a huge weight upon her shoulders pressing her down and she fell upon her knees. Her arms were pulled apart until she was holding them out like the spread wings of a bird. She could not speak.

"Red Bird, Red Bird, Red Bird," Manka cried out, lifting her arms, "Your nest is broken. The Cavern calls. The nest is scattered. The Cavern calls Red Bird. Red Bird, Breath-Changer, leave this body. The Cavern calls!"

Her hands high above her head, she turned her palms downward towards the crouching woman, and Fleay felt a sudden pain at the back of her neck, in her shoulders and along her arms. A shudder ran through her body, and she retched, bent over, her face almost brushing the snow, and then a great weariness came over her and she fell forward, arms still outstretched.

Manka lowered her hands. Her breath was coming in painful gasps.

She crossed her arms upon her breasts and then spread them wide, pulling her cloak apart and letting it fall behind her into the cave.

"Breath is Given, Breath is Taken," she whispered. She bent down, gasping, and pulled fur wrappings off her feet. She stepped down from the stone ledge, and stood naked over Fleay, looking out over the village below her. Her eyes filled with tears. There was a heavy pain in her chest and she could hardly breathe. Darkness was spreading over her eyes.

"Hill-Builder, Womb-Filler, Reed-Breaker," she whispered, "Fire-Breather, Tree-Shaper, Fish-Swimmer, Deer-Caller, Change-Maker, Breath-Singer . . . " Her voice was failing, the darkness growing deeper. "Bird-Hurler, Wolf-Runner, dance in me the Dance . . . " There was nothing but darkness in her eyes now, and the pain itself was a darkness. She felt breath-ending in her but as it did so she whispered through the darkness the last secret words. Fleay lay still, face down in the snow, and felt the words of the whisper brush her back like wings. "Mother, Mother, Mother, help this Change."

○

TWELVE

"At the coming of dark we went," said Gron, "At the coming of dark we return." He looked up at the crest of the hill. "This is the hill of the Cavern," he told Skang. "It is Manka's hill."

He led the way between the outcrops of rock that heaved up from the snow, their flanks glistening with frost, their tops patched with white. He stopped and pointed.

"There will be a burning," he said, and on the top of the other hill they saw a fire beginning.

Plara said quietly, "It is Manka."

Her voice was without feeling; the words were slurred. Gron looked down the hill.

"The Kindred are gathering," he said, "There is the hut fire."

Plara drew herself up. Her voice was stronger. "We make a three-fire," she told them. "We make a three-fire and Dom will shout."

Gron moved more quickly, his fur-clad feet sliding on the thin snow. "Manka, we come," whispered Plara, "Manka, we come."

○

Talker, standing outside his hut, watched the Kindred gather. He fingered his headdress of feathers, and the bones and skull of crow around his neck. "Chooser and Caller and Talker are One," he told himself. He looked up at the Burning Place. He could see the three pillars outlined against the sky that was reddening with the dying sun. Two figures were busy around one of the pillars.

"Manka," he whispered. He put a picture into his head of Manka burning, the flame spurting from her open mouth, the thongs snapping and the body falling into the fire. He smiled to himself and looked up at the sky.

"It is the dark of the dark and the not-women will choose. They will choose as Manka falls into the fire."

He looked again at the Kindred gathering round the hut fire. Fleay was not there. At day-making he had a thinking to pleasure-choose Fleay. Now that thinking was a broken twig. She had come down from the cavern and cried out to all the Kindred, "Manka is gone, Manka is gone!" and the eye-water had been running down her cheeks. Then she had sat by the hut fire and said nothing, rocking her body back and forward, back and forward, a dry reed in the wind. He would not choose Fleay. He would choose a woman who had not been chosen, a short-minded woman with little breasts, a near-woman. He would choose Ganta. He put a picture of Ganta in his head, her thin arms, her big eyes, her soft mouth, her smooth belly, the sparse fur around her fur-hole. He would choose Ganta. Franda had not been chosen. Franda had bigger breasts and fatter arms. He would two-choose. He had a moment's hesitation. He was long-minded and his pleasure-thing was not a strong branch for many breaths. But these were near-women. They would have no thinking.

The Kindred had almost gathered. He could see Fleay. She was sitting on the edge of the circle. She was a thing of stone. There was no fire-breath in her.

He whispered, "Fire-Breath," to himself, and then "Strong-Choosing, Loud-Calling, Fire-Breath." He would lead the gathering from the hut fire to the Burning Place, a great stag leading a herd. He would strike the ground with his staff and he would lead them and they would follow. He would make strong thinkings. He would...

The redness was fading from the sky. There was a heavy cloud above the hills. He sniffed the air. Snow was coming. Not in this breath or in tens and tens of breaths, but it was coming. It would come when the burning was done and Ganta and Franda were with him under the skins and Fleay... Why did a picture of Fleay come to him? He looked at her. She was sitting like a dead stump, not moving. He gripped his staff and went to the gathering.

○

Plara peered and looked round the cavern. It was dark. The fire just inside the opening was no more than a heap of dully glowing ash. She could make out the shapes of things with difficulty, the big pots and the small, the dried meat in the bags of skin, the staff leaning against the wall. Farther inside the cave she could see nothing, not even the small opening to the inner cave where she had never been.

"Here," she said, "I was given the hidden thinkings and the bindings and healings."

Skang stooped to take fuel from the stack of wood.

"No," she told him, "Wait!"

He laid the log back again upon the pile. She stared out of the cavern down at the hut fire where the Kindred had gathered. A tall figure detached itself from the gathering and started on the track up the other hill. The Kindred followed, straggling, in a ragged line.

Gron sniffed the air. "Sky-feathers are coming," he said.

Plara slid out of her cloak. She picked up the one that Manka had discarded and put it on. She took the staff from its place by the wall and held it in her hand. She smiled to herself. Skang and Gron stared.

"Manka is not gone," she said. Her face seemed to shine in the near-darkness, and her eyes were bright. "It is Change," she said, "and this is the thinking. . . . "

○

"The Cavern is empty. The Cavern is cold," said Talker. He lifted his staff. "She who was Outer-Thing and Not Outer-Thing, she who was not of the Kindred, she who kept the Kindred away from the Cavern, she who took away hurtings that the Kindred would bring her meat and drink, but gave the Kindred breath-endings, is gone."

Bode shouted, "She did not give breath-endings; she was the helper."

Talker struck the ground with his staff. "To Henda she gave breath-ending, to Caller she gave breath-ending, to Skelda she gave breath-ending," he shouted. "She was of the Womb and fed the Womb breath-endings."

There was a shocked silence. "In this dark of the dark a strong thinking comes," cried Talker, "Here in the Burning Place is the Cavern. It is the Cavern and the Womb. Here I make the Cavern and the Womb."

He lifted his staff and laid it across the two standing stones.

"A big stone will be put here," he said, "and this will be the Cavern and the Womb-Opening, and the place of Fire-Breath. Is it Chosen?"

Before the spear carriers could shout their response, Fleay, seated far from the fire, seeming to wake from a stupor, cried out, "Let the Fire-Breath speak!" Talker took the staff down from the stones and struck it on the ground. "The Fire-Breath will speak. Make the fire," he called.

Fire-Maker took up the long stick with the bundle of twigs thonged to it and thrust it into the flames. Fleay leaned forward. The mist had cleared from her head. She felt a lightness in her body. Her fingers tingled. As the torch plunged into the pile of wood beneath the body tied to the pillar and the flames took hold she heard words in her head, words that were new to her, and yet words she had heard before.

"Mother, Mother, Mother help this Change," she repeated to herself as the flames, crackling and sputtering, rose, and the hair became flame; then, as a tongue of fire leapt from the gaping mouth, she heard, in Manka's voice, as if Manka was crying from the cloak of fire, "The Cavern Calls."

She rose to her feet and shouted, "The Cavern Calls!"

Talker lost his grip on his staff, but grabbed it before it could fall.

"The fire speaks!" he shouted, but Fleay had turned her back and was pointing, and, there on the hill where the cavern was, they saw a fire. Three tongues of flame leapt up from that fire into the air and sped towards them. The burning of Manka was forgotten. Craning, they watched the streaks of fire hurtle through the sky above them and scattered wildly as they fell. "Fire-spears," gasped Bode, as they struck the earth, "Fire-spears that fly like birds."

"It is the Fire-Breath," Talker shouted, "It brings the fire from the Cavern to the Cavern, from the cold womb to the Womb I have made. The fire has spoken."

The Kindred turned and looked at him and at the pillar of fire. The thongs were burning, and as they broke, the body slumped down into the flames.

"Is it Chosen?" shouted Talker. "Is it Chosen?"

The spear carriers hesitated a moment and then through the smoke-heavy air came a sound as of drumming hooves, a sound as of ice breaking, of trees cracking, of stone upon stone, growing ever louder. The sound came from the Cavern. The Kindred huddled together. Talker dropped his staff and staggered. Arms outstretched, he braced himself between the two stones.

Maker, his eyes upon the Burning-Stone, cried out "It breaks!"

There was a sound like a thunderclap as the pillar split top to bottom, and the two halves fell away. Fire-Maker looked up and screamed. The greater half was falling towards her. Maker leapt over her and put his hands to the stone. For the space of half a breath he seemed to hold it, and Fire-Maker rolled away. Then his arms buckled, and the stone, twisting as it fell, crashed to the earth. He gave a cry of pain, and the astonished and frightened Kindred saw that though his body had been spared the stone had fallen upon his hands.

There was a groan from the whole Gathering. Talker tried to speak, but could not. Fleay, her face stiff, walked through the Gathering and stood before Talker. She bent down and picked up his staff. The Kindred waited.

"It is *not* Chosen," she said, "And no one of the Kindred will choose this dark, no woman, no not-woman. The talk is over. In Her Womb we lie this dark, and in our bodies She keeps Her presence."

She looked at the staff in her hand as if bemused and turned and gave it back to Talker. She lifted her face to the sky. "The sky-feathers are falling," she said matter of factly and a few big flakes of snow drifted down. Slowly she walked to the opening, the Kindred making way for her, and then following her down the hill.

○

"The Great Change is coming," said Plara.

She put more wood on the fire. The fire on the other hill was no more than a dull glow.

"The Kindred will not come in the dark," she said, "and this is the dark of dark, and the sky-feathers fall thickly from the white bird."

She went to the back of the cave, feeling her way. "There is a big pot of the fire-keeper that we put on the arrows," she said. "We will put it on short branches and go through the opening to the womb beyond the womb."

She found the pot and brought it to the fire. "It is tree-sweat and black wood dust," she said, and picked three stout branches from the wood pile. "I make the bud," she said, folding the substance round the end of the short branches, "and the bud will flower." She thrust the end of one branch into the fire and there was a bright flame. "Now," she said, "we meet what is hidden," and led the way to the back of the cave.

Once through the opening they found themselves in a narrow passage; the walls shone in the flare of the torches and were smooth and cold to the touch. Beneath their fur-clad feet the earth was firmly packed down, but after a few paces it gave way to rock. The passage sloped downwards at first and then, after a twist, they found themselves climbing. They heard, faintly, the sound of running water. Plara, in the front, said "It is here," and moved quickly ahead. Gron and Skang hurried after her. They were standing in a huge cave. They walked round the walls towards the sound of running water, and discovered a pool and, beyond it, another opening in the rock. They stared into the pool but could see only the quivering flames of their torches.

"The water runs away here," said Gron, having moved away from them. "It goes down into the deep of the hill."

Plara walked round the pool and, bending, peered into the farther opening.

"The pool fills from here," she said, and holding the torch in front of her, dropped upon her knees and crawled up the little stream. Skang made to follow her, but Gron held him back. They waited a long time. At last they saw a glimmer of light in the opening and then the full flare of the torch with Plara's face behind it, her eyes shining. She stood up and held the torch high.

"There is a two-pool," she said, her voice hushed with the surprise of it, "and it is a Watching Pool. Beyond the pool there is a deep. I threw a stone. I did not hear it again. It is the deep of the Womb. The water comes into the Watching Pool from high on the cavern wall, and where it comes there is a mark. It is a mark like a fur-hole. There is a pleasure-thing in it."

She said, "Moons gone, the Taken were of this place, and the Taken pleasure-chose!"

Gron laughed. There was an echo. Skang walked into the middle of the cave. "Ho," he shouted and "Ho Ho Oho" the echo returned.

"Dom would speak loud in here," he said.

"Dom would make Dance here," Plara said suddenly, "Bring the fire flowers." She was staring at one of the walls. "Look," she said. "There are marks."

They stared. There were many marks. "They are women," said Gron. "Here are legs and arms and here are breasts. They are dancing," he said.

Plara pointed lower down. "It is round, but round as ripples are when a stone is thrown in the pool," she said, "or round as a basket is round when the reeds are woven. It is a dancing round. It is the Dance." She gave a little jump of excitement. "Here is the dancing place," she cried, and "Dancing place, -ing place, place, -ace" the cavern responded. She lowered the torch.

"It comes to me that tens and tens of moons gone, tens and more tens than there can be thinkings, there were many Taken. It was not one-woman and two-woman. This was in Manka's deep-mind and she gave me the happening. This is the place of the Taken, the dancing place."

Gron stared around him. "All the Kindred could dance here," he said in awe, "and all the giftings and . . . . . " His voice trailed away.

"There is water," said Skang, and then he sniffed. "There is good breath," he said. "The fire-breath goes up. It goes away."

They stared up at the roof. "Dance in me the Dance," murmured Plara. "Dance in Womb, the Womb inside the Womb. Dance in the Womb."

She gave a sudden small cry and put her hand on her belly. "It dances," she said. "It dances! The birth dances." She laughed.

Gron said, "I will bring Dom."

"No," said Plara. "Go to the fire and wait. I will watch in the Watching Pool. Then I will come."

She went through the tiny opening, crawling up the shallow dark stream, and into the small cave. There she knelt down by the pool and peered into it, her torch held out over the water. "It is Manka," she said softly. "It is Manka and Plara." The waters of the pool moved darkly under her gaze.

○

"The sky-feathers do not fall," said Fire-Maker, pulling aside the skins on the opening of Maker's hut. She turned back and crouched beside Maker, not daring to touch his broken and swollen hands. Maker stared up at her.

"It came to Manka," he said. "It was a picture in her head. My hands were broken. It is a big hurting."

Fire-Maker held the little pot of drink to his lips.

"There is not one of the Kindred to take the hurting away," said Maker. "I am Broken-Fingered, Stiff-Wristed, Not-Maker and Manka has gone."

Fire-Maker put the pot aside. "It is Bode's thinking that Manka has not gone," she said. "It has come to Bode that Manka has returned to the Cavern. You must go to Manka. She will take away the hurting."

Maker nodded slowly. "I will go," he said.

○

Fleay crouched by the hut-fire. She smiled to herself. Her head felt light and empty. There was warmth in all her body. She looked at her hands. "Not hooks, not spears, not claws," she whispered. She felt herself giggling. Two not-women squatted down beside the fire. She glanced at them with indifference, and the giggle inside her became stronger. She threw back her head and laughed aloud.

"You laugh?" said Prand. "What picture is in your head?"

"I have no picture," said Fleay, "I have no thinking," but as she spoke she saw herself standing by the Watching Pool and her Other was looking up at her and smiling, and "Yes," she said, aloud, "Yes," and rose to her feet. "I go to the Cavern," she said.

Delk gaped at her. "The Cavern is empty," he said. "The fire has come to the Burning Place. That is the Cavern and the Womb. It was in the Fire-Breath." Fleay said nothing. She pointed. A fire was flickering in the mouth of the Cavern. She laughed again.

"I give you this thinking," she said. "Take it to Talker. When the net is broken a new net is made."

○

"We will go to the Cavern," said Bode firmly. Freng and Polla shifted uneasily on their feet. Polla said nervously, "You are ever-minded?" Bode said, "It was from Manka. A woman finds breath-ending and is burned but her womb brings birth to one and two and three. We go to the three." Freng stared up at the cavern with narrowed eyes. "I see no three," she said. "I see fire. I do not see three." "You must look into the basket to see the berries," said Bode. "We will go."

○

" . . . And she goes to the Cavern," said Delk.

Talker picked up his staff and went out of the hut.

"Maker and Fire-Maker go," said Prand, pointing, "and Bode, Polla, Freng."

"There are Three!" shouted Delk. "Look!"

Outside the Cavern stood three still figures outlined against the snow.

"A woman and two not-women," said Prand.

Talker gripped his staff until the knuckles were white. "Manka was Outer-Thing. The Cavern is the place of outer-things. These are outer-things," he said. "Call Harn. Call the Protector. Call the spear carriers."

○

Plara stood between the two men and looked down at the Kindred coming up the hill. Skang wore the mask of the white wolf upon his head and the forepaws were around his neck. He held a bow, and there were arrows at his side. Gron wore crow feathers in his air. Dom was slung about his neck and he held a stick in each hand. Plara, in Manka's cloak, holding Manka's staff, was dwarfed between them. She licked her dry lips.

"There are six and there are ten," said Gron, narrowing his eyes. "The six are five women and one not-woman. The ten are not-women with spears. The ten are shouting. They run."

Skang fitted an arrow to his bow. "One does not run," he said, "the one with a big staff and feathers upon his head and bones around his neck."

"It is Talker," said Gron. "He is long-minded and cannot run."

"They are shouting 'Outer-Thing'," said Gron. He cocked his head to listen. "They are shouting 'Breath-ending to the outer-things'."

"They have passed by the six. The big not-woman leads the pack. He has teeth and claws round his neck," said Skang.

"Harn," muttered Gron.

Plara said, "Let Dom speak!" and a sound like far thunder rolled from the cavern, and then a coughing slapping sound, a sound of trees breaking in the big wind. The nine men stopped running. They looked up at the Cavern. Talker, from behind them, shouted, "Outer-things! It is the sound of outer-things! Breath-ending to outer-things that bring breath-endings to the Kindred! Spear! Spear!"

The spear carriers gave a great cry and ran forward up the hill, Harn leading them. He held his spear high above his head, poised to throw.

Plara said, "Dom be still! Wolf, leap!" and Skang raised his bow and loosed the arrow. Harn threw up his hands; his spear flew off into the snow, and a bubbling scream burst from his throat. He fell backwards. The spear carriers scattered.

"The outer-things are three," shouted Talker, "and the Kindred are many. Breath-ending to the outer-things! Spear! Spear!"

The spear carriers hesitated.

"Send a one-hurting and a two-hurting," said Plara softly.

Skang raised his bow again, and the two men fell with arrows in their thighs. Gron did not wait to be told. Once more thunder rolled and trees broke apart and tens and tens of hooves hammered the dry ground.

Plara stepped a pace forward. Her voice was sharp and clear. "In Her, Through Her, this happening," she cried.

"It is Manka and Not-Manka," whispered Bode, "It is Wolf and Kraw and the spears as quick as a bird."

Polla, peering, said, "Kraw is Gron that found breath-ending. Gron has come back from the Womb. In Her, Through Her," she muttered, crossing her arms upon her breast.

The two groups of the Kindred were now one, for the spear carriers had fallen back, the two wounded leaning upon others. In front of them in the snow lay the body of Harn, the snow around him crimson.

Prand said, "It is not Manka. It is Twig-Legged Stiff-Walker, it is little Plara."

Bode shaded her eyes with her hand. "It is Manka and Not-Manka, and it is Plara," she said. She frowned, in puzzlement. Plara stood watching them, leaning upon her staff, her belly thrust forward. "She has a big belly," said Bode. "She will make birth."

"Plara was Taken," said Polla. "The Taken do not make birth. The Taken who make birth are outer-things."

"And she has pleasure-chosen," said Talker quickly, "She has two-chosen. There are the not-women at her side." He raised his voice.

"Plara was Taken and has pleasure-chosen," he shouted. "She is an outer-thing."

There was a rumble of agreement among the spear carriers. Fleay turned on them.

"Talker is Talker," she spat, "He is not Chooser. He is not Caller. There is no Chooser. There is no Caller." She grabbed Maker's arm and held it up high. "There is no Maker," she cried, and, pointing at the corpse of Harn, "There is no Protector. There is only Talker." Her voice was scornful. "There is Talker, Talker, Talker," she cried, "and Talker is White-Haired Wide-Mouthed Body-Earth-Maker."

Talker, trembling with fury, swung at her with his staff and knocked her to the ground. She lay there a moment, then raised herself on one elbow.

"Kindred do not strike Kindred," she said. "Talker is Outer-Thing."

Talker stepped backwards. His mouth opened. No sound emerged. Then he rose to his full height. "Gather! Gather!" he cried. "There is a Gathering. I am ever-minded and it comes to me that in the Gathering there will be strong thinkings and there will be Change."

Bode helped Fleay to her feet. "You are not Caller," she spat.

Talker turned his back on her and went down the hill. The spear carriers followed. The body of Harn lay forgotten in the snow.

O

THIRTEEN

The six stood uneasily before the mouth of the cavern. Bode was the first to speak.

"It is the picture that came to Manka," she said, "Wolf and Kraw and the sky-feathers of the white bird and the bird-spear. But there was a tree that walked and ran."

Gron held out Dom and struck it gently.

"Ah," said Bode, "You are Manka and Not-Manka and you are Plara the Taken."

"I am Plara the Taken. The three are Taken, Plara, Gron, and Skang."

Bode frowned. "There is a strong thinking that not-women are not Taken, that the Taken do not choose, and do not make birth. Here are three twigs that are broken."

Plara sighed. She sat down on the ledge of rock. "The strong thinkings are of the Kindred. We are not of the Kindred. We are of the Cavern. There is Change."

Fleay said, "I was Taken and Not-Taken. There was a red bird in me. My hands were hooks and spears. My tongue was a knife. Manka took away the red bird. Talker struck me with his staff. I am not of the Kindred. Am I of the Cavern?"

Plara stared into her eyes. "In the Watching Pool I saw the face of Fleay. You are of the Cavern."

"I have not been Taken," said Bode, "but I am not of the Kindred. I am of Manka and Not-Manka. I am of the Cavern."

Plara said nothing.

"I am of Bode," said Polla, her lip jutting with determination.

"And I am of Bode," said Freng.

Plara looked at Fire-Maker. Fire-Maker said hesitantly, "I am not Fire-Maker. I am Slow-Tongued Twig-Gatherer. I have no thinking, but Maker has a big hurting."

"I will take it away," said Plara. "In ten darks there will be no hurting."

Maker said, "There is a strong thinking that not-women are not Taken. Tens and tens and tens of moons gone I saw my Other, and pictures came into my head, and I struck stone with stone. It was In Her Through Her I found the making." He paused. "On the burning stone there are marks. They were from Her. They were not my thinking. It comes to me that She broke the stone. I am not of the Kindred."

Fire-Maker put her arm round his shoulders. "I am of Maker," she said.

Gron, still standing, pointed down the hill. "The Kindred gather," he said, "Do you go to the Gathering?"

Fleay said, "I will go."

Fire-Maker, her arm still around Maker, said, "Maker has a hurting. I am of Maker."

Bode looked first at Polla then at Vlenk.

"We will go to the Gathering," she said grimly. "We will carry the body of Harn to the Gathering."

Plara picked up her staff and rose to her feet. "I am heavy-bellied," she said. "My belly that was small is big. Her belly that was small is big. It is as big as many huts. Those that are of the Cavern will find eating and drinking and sleeping in Her womb."

○

"This is a hut-gathering," said Talker. "At the coming of dark there will be a burning and Fire-Breath will choose the thinkings."

He gazed at the Kindred seated round the fire. The spear carriers were together in one place, the spear blades pointing upwards at the

146

grey sky. "I am ever-minded from near-sleep," he said, "and strong thinkings are in my head. They are new strong thinkings and of the Kindred. The strong thinkings of moons gone were of the Cavern. They were of Manka. Manka, the Outer-Thing, put thinkings into the head of Chooser and Caller, and Chooser is Log-Woman and Caller has found breath-ending. Manka has burned and the new strong thinkings are of the Kindred." He leaned on his staff.

Bode leaned forward. "Moons gone there was a strong thinking that no spears come to the hut-gathering," she said. "There are spears."

"It was a thinking of the Cavern," said Talker. "Not-women are the spear carriers. Manka was woman. It is a twig that has broken."

"Moons gone," said Bode, "women carried spears."

"That is a stone dropped in the pool," said Talker. "It will not see the sky again." He struck the ground with his staff. "It is the spear carriers that bring deer meat and bear meat. It is the spear carriers that move the big stones and the spear carriers that run quick and leap high and have strong in them. It comes to me that in this dark of dark and in this coming moon and in all moons that come the not-women will choose and the women will be chosen. This is the strong thinking that the Fire-Breath will choose."

"That Talker will choose," spat Polla. "It is not Fire-Breath, but Talker-Breath."

"There are spears," said Talker softly, "and spears give hurtings. Protector is a not-woman. I call Drong Protector."

Drong went through the gathering and stood beside Talker. The necklace of teeth and claws that had been Harn's was hung around his neck.

"Is it Chosen?"

"It is Chosen."

"Fire-Maker is a woman. I call Ganta Fire-Maker. Is it Chosen?"

"It is Chosen."

Ganta, thin-armed, shyly moved to the fire in front of Talker. She was trembling.

"Ganta is near-woman," objected Spella, her eyes angry, "She has spilled no blood from her fur-hole."

Talker ignored her. "Maker is not-woman," he said. "I call Grek. He will make a burning stone that will not break, and a three-stone for the Womb opening. Is it Chosen?"

"It is Chosen."

Grek stood up. "It is not Chosen," he said. "I make In Her, Through Her, and it comes to me from the ever-mind that it was through Her that the burning stone broke Maker's hands. My hands will make no burning stone. I am Knife-Handed Stone-Striker. I am not Maker."

Talker bit his lip. He glanced at Drong. "Drong is Protector," he said. "He will protect. With his spear." Drong lifted his spear.

Grek said, "The spear of Drong is quick. The bird-spear is quicker." He smiled. "She is in the Cavern. She will send bird-spears and Drong will find breath-ending."

"There are three outer-things in the Cavern," said Talker, "and there are ten-and-ten spear carriers. It comes to me that ten-and-ten spear carriers are a big wind that breaks three trees."

"It comes to me," said Bode, "that there is no Maker and there is no Chooser and there is no Caller and this is not a Gathering."

"Maker is Chosen," said Talker, "and Fire-Breath is Chooser and Caller."

"Fire-Breath is Wide-Mouthed Body-Earth-Maker," said Vlenk. "Fire-Breath is Talker, is pebbles in an empty pot."

Grek, still on his feet, said firmly. "I make In Her, Through Her, and not in Fire-Breath."

He looked round at the gathering. "And I am not Maker," he said.

There was a muttering among the spear carriers. Karn stood. "I am not of Fire-Breath, I am of Her," he said, "I will not pleasure-choose."

Talker drew his breath in sharply. He smiled a thin smile. "There are deer that run and deer that leap," he said, "there are Kindred that choose and Kindred that do not. This is a dry leaf on the tree."

Fleay rose to her feet. "It comes to me," she said, "That Talker and Chooser and Caller are in one body, and there is a strong thinking that what is Chosen and called is a thong that binds the Kindred. There is a strong thinking that the hand and knife that cut that thong are the hand and knife of an outer-thing, and outer-things go from the Kindred. There is no thinking where outer-things go. At day-making there were three in the Cavern. At this time of gathering there are five. I break the thong that is on the Kindred and I go to the Cavern." She made her way slowly through the huddle of Kindred.

Bode rose. "I am not of the Kindred," she said. "I am of the Cavern.

In Her, Through Her." She turned and looked at Grek. Grek rose, and Karn.

"There are ten-and-eight spear carriers," said Bode.

"Seven," said Krill.

He stood. Polla and Vlenk stood also. Two women with babies in their arms also stood up. Talker struck the ground with his staff. "The Talk is not over," he shouted. "The Gathering is not over. There are spears!"

Fleay, at the edge of the Gathering turned and stretched her arms up high. She threw back her head. "Mother, Mother, Mother," she called, the words coming to her from far away darkness, "Mother, Mother, Mother, help this Change!" She lowered her hands and shook her head stupidly. She gazed across the gathering and said very softly, "Ganta." Ganta ran to her. Talker, roaring with fury, grabbed the spear from Drong and hurled it over the heads of the startled Gathering. Fleay cried out and fell.

○

The fire blazed brightly in the big cave, the smoke rising straight and steadily up the roof and through the small hole. From the cracks in the cave walls jutted torches.

"There was a burning?" asked Bode. Memma nodded.

"They burned Harn," she said, "But there was no burning stone. He burned in the fire. The Kindred were all there. Talker stood between the stones, and Drong stood at his side."

"Not at the opening?"

"The spear carriers were at the opening. Drong stood by Talker." She shook the melting snow from her cloak and moved closer to the fire. Gron came into the cave with Karn. They carried a pig between them strung on a pole.

"The big gifting," said Gron. "The sky-feathers are thick. We cannot get another."

Plara, bending over Maker, said, "The Kindred will not come with spears if the sky-feathers are falling. I have a thinking that Skang and Grek come into the big cave."

"I take the thinking," said Karn and went back through the passage.

"Talker had a strong thinking," Memma hurried on, "and it was a thick twig to break." She giggled. "He had a picture in his head, and it had come from Fire-Breath. It was a picture of one big tree and there were no bushes. The Tree spread its branches over all the huts and berries fell from it into the mouths of the Kindred. On the one-branch were leaves and the leaves were spear carriers and Protector was the branch. On the two-branch there were pots and baskets and stone knives and spears and the branch was Maker. And on the three-branch the leaves were fire-makers and food-makers and that branch was Woman-branch."

"Maker?" asked Grek, newly come in from the outer cave, "Is there a Maker?"

"It is Frin," giggled Memma, "It is Reed-Wristed Slow-Walker." Grek laughed. "The twig did not break," said Memma. "The spear carriers did not choose. Then Drong had a thinking." She giggled again. "He saw the picture of the tree. He saw the Maker branch and the Woman branch and the trunk of the tree was the spear carriers and the trunk was the spear-carrier branch, and the tree was Protector. He had a strong thinking that Protector was chosen big tree, and he shouted, 'Is it Chosen,' and it was Chosen."

"Protector is Chooser, Caller, Talker?"

"Protector, Chooser and Caller are one body. The body has a short-calling. It is Leader."

"But Talker?" asked Krill.

Memma rocked back and forward with laughter. "Fire-Breath is Fire-Maker. It was the thinking of Drong that Talker was of the fire. It was a big happening."

"Did the not-women pleasure-choose that dark?" asked Grek.

Memma stopped smiling. "They chose," she said. "They two-chose. They chose women and near-women. Three not-women chose Kanta who has spilled no blood from her fur-hole."

"And Memma?" asked Plara gently.

"Drong, and Bundi, and Farn and Skall," whispered Memma. "Pren did not pleasure-choose." She lifted her head, her eyes wet. "I am not of the Kindred," she said, "I am of the Cavern. I chose Pren but Drong... chose." Bode put her arms around her. "At day-making I came," said Memma. "The sky-feathers were falling. Skall was in sleep. By the hut fire was Pren. There was a spear in him."

○

Talker huddled beside the hut fire. The snow was falling thickly, and the fire spat and sputtered. The Kindred were in their huts, and had made smaller fires in the hut openings. He reached back into his long-mind. He had no picture of so heavy a fall of sky-feathers. "It is the year of the white bird," he told himself. His bones ached. He stood and walked round the fire, stamping his feet. There was a pain in his chest. Fire-Helper had not come. He dragged another log from the pile under the covering of skins and carried it to the fire. The log was heavy. He looked up the hill. He could not see the Cavern. He could not see the Burning Place.

○

"This is the one-Gathering in the dark of the dark," said Plara. "I have stood at the Watching Pool and I have seen."

"You are Chooser?" asked Polla.

Plara smiled. "I am Round-Bellied Pool-Watcher," she said, "and I am Plara. It came to me in near-sleep at the Watching Pool. There is Change. The strong thinkings of the Kindred are broken twigs. These are the strong thinkings of the Cavern.

"The one-strong thinking is of Chooser. There is no Chooser. The women of the Cavern are Chooser. The women enter the ever-mind and choose the strong thinkings. Six choose and three do not choose: it is Chosen. One chooses and two do not choose: it is not Chosen."

"Three choose. Three do not choose?" queried Bode.

"It is not Chosen," said Plara, "and these are the strong thinkings the women will choose or will not choose. There is a strong thinking that all of the Cavern will have bird-spears and that Skang will give the happenings that make them."

"Skang is Protector?"

"The women will choose Protector at the new knife moon; when there is a new knife moon there will be a new Protector. The Protector is a woman."

"Women carry no spears," said Bode.

"It is the thinking that women carry spears and bird-spears," said Plara.

The Gathering was silent. "It is Change," said Delk. "It is big Change."

"You go to the Kindred?" asked Plara.

Delk shook his head. "I am of Change, I am of the Cavern."

"Caller, Maker, Fire-Maker?" asked Bode impatiently. "The women choose Fire-Maker for one day and one dark. At the Gathering the women choose. The women choose Caller for one moon."

"Maker?" queried Polla.

"Maker is Maker," said Plara. "He is of the Taken. I take away his hurtings."

"The burnings," whispered Memma, "the burnings, the pleasure-choosings?"

Plara said, "There are no burnings. Those that find breath-ending return to the deep of the Womb." She pointed across the Cavern. "In that place is the Watching Pool and across the Watching Pool is a track through rock and into the hill and the track finds ending in a great fall into the dark. Two of the Taken will carry the body."

"The pleasure-choosings?" insisted Memma. "The choosings?"

"The pleasure-choosing will be one-choosing. The women will choose."

"There are ten-and-ten women and ten not-women," said Grek, "and five near-women."

Plara said, "The women will choose, some one dark, some another dark. Caller will take those fish from the river. At the five dark there will be no choosing."

Bode leaned forward. "The Taken choose?" she said.

Plara nodded. "The Taken choose and are chosen," she said. "Women and not-women are Taken. Plara is Taken, and Gron, and Skang and Maker."

Bode pointed to a dark corner of the Cavern. "Is Fleay Taken?"

"She is Taken," said Plara.

○

"Ten-and-nine women have gone to the Cavern," said Kand, "and five near-women."

Drong frowned. "They went through the thick sky-feathers," said Kand, "and they took the short-minded and the breast-nuzzlers, and they took Log-Woman that was Chooser." He bit his thumb anxiously.

"And the not-women?" asked Drong.

"Krill, Grek, Delk, Benk, Skard, Gurn, Dend have gone," Drong shouted. "Fire-Maker, Prand, Grek, are white-haired, long-minded, twig-legged," he said. "Here are ten and four not-women that have strong in them. And the women?"

Kand grunted. "There are ten and one," he said. "Two are long-minded and give no pleasuring."

Drong grunted. He looked outside the hut. "The sky-feathers fall," he said, "In the Cavern are ten not-women. In the Kindred are ten-and-four. The Kindred have no bird-spears. We will find breath-ending."

Kand leaned forward. "Talker," he said. He corrected himself. "Fire-Maker," he said, "has strong thinkings."

Drong scratched himself. "The sky-feathers fall," he muttered. "They fall into my head. I have no thinkings."

"Fire-Maker," urged Kand.

"Bring," said Drong.

○

Fleay pushed at the waters. Her arms were briars. They bent and twisted. She was in the pool. She was in the Watching Pool. She was Other and Fleay was calling. She opened her mouth. She thrust with her feet. Her feet were the roots of trees. She was a tree under the water. She had branches. The briars were branches. She thrust them up through the water. Fleay was calling to the Other. Fleay was the Other. There was a fire-worm in her shoulder. It broke. There were two fire-worms. There were three. There were four. They were small fire-worms. They were smalling. They were small. They were sparks of fire and the briars were branches. She reached up. She would bud. She would blossom. Her hands were above the water; her head was above the water. it was Fleay looking down at her. "I am the Other," she whispered. "I am the Other," and the face was not the face of Fleay but of Plara. The words were of Plara.

"You are the bird I send," whispered Plara, "You are the bird I send."

Fleay opened her eyes. The cavern was shadowed and quiet but for the small noises of sleep.

"I have taken away the hurting," said Plara.

Fleay nodded. Her shoulder ached but the fire-worms had gone.

"You are the bird I send," whispered Plara. "You are the bird I send to the Kindred." Fleay stared at her. "You are your Other," said Plara, "You are Taken. I send you to Talker."

Fleay shuddered. "Talker? That is gone."

"The fish swims but the hook is in the fish," said Plara. "There is a picture to put into the head of Talker. It is the Change that is In Her, Through Her, and it is of the Kindred and of the Cavern."

Fleay lay back. "I will send the bird," she said.

○

"There are two pictures in my head," said Talker. "I am Fire-Maker and they come to me in Fire-Breath." He coughed. Kand gave him a pot of drink. Drong scowled. "The sky-feathers do not fall. The stiff-water is wet and grows soft. The Kindred gather at the hut fire. There are no women in the Kindred. They have gone to the cavern." He sipped on the drink.

Drong said harshly, "The two-picture?"

"The Kindred are in a green place. The sky-feathers do not fall. The stiff-water is soft. There are deer in the trees and Paeg. There is no cavern." He bent forward. "There are no short-minded ones in the picture but there are women and breast nuzzlers, and there are bushes with berries."

"Is there Drong?"

Talker stared at him.

"There is Drong," he said. He put his hand to his head. "It comes to me. It comes from the ever-mind. I see Drong and the spear carriers of the Kindred and the women of the Kindred and it is a new knife moon and they are going from the huts. They are going through the trees. They are going far."

He stopped suddenly. He stared wildly into the air between them.

"I do not see the long-minded," he said. "There are no long-minded." He bowed his head in his hands. "I do not see Fire-Maker," he whispered.

Drong grunted. He lifted his hand and struck out.

"Look! Look!" he commanded.

Talker lifted his head. "Green place," he muttered, "Deer. Paeg. Tens and Tens. No Cavern," and then with a sudden access of energy, "There is strong in it. There are big huts and ten-and-ten-and-ten of women and Leader." His eyes narrowed. "There is Leader," he said. "The Kindred go from the huts and there is Leader."

○

Plara knelt by the Watching Pool. The torch flame flickered and then stilled, a thin thread of smoke rising straight upwards. Plara bowed her head. "Mother," she said, "this dark is new knife moon. You have Taken Memma. You have Taken Farla. Grek comes to You. In You, Through You. The Kindred do not come to the giftings. It is in their heads that there are bird-spears that give breath-endings and the giftings are of You and You are of the Cavern. The Kindred are not of the Cavern." She took a deep breath. "I come to the Other that is In You, Through You. I am my Other In You, Through You."

She opened her eyes and stared into the water. The face that stared up at her was grave. There were lines on its forehead. The lips were firm. A ripple ran over the face and then another and a third. It was no longer a face but a cavern. There were people in the cavern. Plara peered. They were seated around a fire. There were women and not-women and near-women and small ones. It was no longer a cavern. There were stone huts around the people.

As Plara watched, the people rose to their feet. One of them pointed into the sky, and the people melted away and Plara was looking at the full round of the moon. The moon grew bigger and brighter. It filled her head. Then it broke into tens and tens of pieces. She heard the sound of Dom thumping steadily as the thump of the heart, and the cavern was before her again, and the people were standing round a fire and moving their arms and legs. The sound of Dom grew faster. The people were throwing up their hands. The fire grew brighter. It filled the cavern. There were no people. The fire was red. Everything was red. It was a sky all over red. The sun rose into the sky. The huts lay quiet under the sun. The people came out of the huts. One woman looked upward. She crossed her arms upon her breast then flung them wide. By her feet lay Wolf. On her shoulder perched Kraw. She moved away from the people. She was rising through the waters of the pool. The pool was again a cavern and the face that stared up at Plara was the face of her Other. The face was smiling.

Plara rose stiffly to her feet. She slid awkwardly into the passage to the great cave, her head filled still with the sound of Dom. The cave was filled with shadow. Light filtering down from the hole that let out the fire-breath left the edges of the cavern dark. The people were seated in small groups, talking as they worked.

Gron came in from the outer cave. He stood still for a moment, then he cried out, "The sky-feathers no longer fall. Skang and Bode and Polla have gone to the giftings with bird-spears in their hands, and the Kindred are leaving." He came further into the cavern and stood by the fire. "The women carry meat and skins and pots," he said. "The not-women carry spears. The skins in the hut-openings are pulled down. The hut-fire is dark." He stared round excitedly. "In Her, Through Her this Change," he cried, "In Her, Through Her."

○

"This dark of the new knife moon the women have Chosen," said Bode. She looked round at the gathering. "The women are Chooser. Bode is not Chooser. She is the voice of Chooser." She paused. "The strong thinkings of Plara are chosen," she said. "Maker is Maker. Memma is Fire-Maker this dark. Fleay is Caller this moon. Bode is Protector this moon. It is Chosen. Is it Called?"

Fleay stood up. "It is Chosen and Called."

Bode said, "The women went into the ever-mind, the women who are Taken and the women who are Not-Taken. In the ever-mind we saw Manka and Manka gave us a strong thinking. It came to us that there are three stones at the opening. There is the one-stone that is Gron. There is the two-stone that is Skang. There is the three-stone over them and it is Plara."

Plara stood. "The one- and two- and three-stones are of the Kindred not of the Cavern," she said. "Skang is Skang and Wolf and Bird-Spear. Gron is Gron and Kraw and Dom. Plara is Plara."

"Plara is Talker," said Bode. "It is Chosen."

Plara held up her hand. "Dom is Talker," she said and turned to Gron. Gron took up the two sticks. There was a slow thrumming as of a heart beat.

"Hill-Builder," called Plara, "Womb-Filler, Reed-Breaker." The drumming quickened. It was the sound of deer hooves on hard ground. "Fire-Breather-Tree-Shaper, Fish-Swimmer," cried Plara, and the drumming was the sound of trees breaking, of branches falling. "Deer-Caller, Change-Maker, Breath-Singer." The drumming was thunder. It rolled around the cavern. Memma stood up. Greng stood. The people were all standing. "Bird-Hurler, Wolf-Runner," cried Plara, on her feet, her hands moving above her head, and the drumbeat was the movement of her hands and the movement of her feet. *"Dance in me the Dance!"* she cried, and the people were all moving their hands and their feet, and the drumbeat echoed in the cavern.

"The moon is round. The womb is round," cried Plara, "Make round the womb," and, shuffling and stamping, she began to move round the fire.

"The womb is round," shouted Bode and followed her, stamping and waving.

"The womb is round," echoed Polla.

"The womb is round. We fill the womb," cried Plara, her hair swinging from side to side.

"Stretch the bow," cried Skang suddenly, making the movement with his arms, and "Stretch the bow," cried Shalla.

"Haul the net," cried Grek, bowing forward and hauling with his hands.

"Pick the berries," cried little Ganta clawing at the air with her hands.

"Stone on stone," shouted Maker from his seat pile of furs and "Stone on stone" came the answering cry. The drumbeat slowed once more to a steady pulse-beat.

"In Her, Through Her," called Plara. "In Her, Through Her" came the response, the people moving more slowly round the fire. The drumbeat slowed further, became quiet. Plara lowered her voice, "Strong is in the Cavern," she cried. "Warm is in the Cavern. She is in the Cavern."

The dance had almost stopped. The people were scarcely moving.

"It is new knife moon," said Plara, "At day-making there are huts for the people. It is breath-beginning. It is birth." She lowered her hands to her sides. "The talk is over."

"It is well," said Bode.

Fleay stepped out of the circle. She stared at Plara and then at the gathering stock-still round the fire. Her voice cracked. "In Her womb we lie this dark, and in our bodies She keeps Her presence."

Gron lifted his sticks one more time and the thunder rolled round the cavern, and in the belly of Plara the child Danced.

OOO

Fires of the Kindred

Edited and designed by Dianna Painter
Cover art and design by Soren Henrich
Typeset in Pilgrim 10/13 at the Typeworks, Vancouver, B. C.
Printed in Canada on 60lb Hi-bulk Offset at Hignell Printing
Limited, Winnipeg, Manitoba.

Other speculative fiction published by Porcépic Books:

Tesseracts, *Judith Merril, Ed.*
  isbn 0-88878-242-X
Tesseracts², *Douglas Barbour & Phyllis Gotlieb, Eds.*
  isbn 0-88878-270-5
The Adventures of Roberta, *by Munro Ferguson*
  isbn 0-88878-241-1
Your Time My Time, *by Ann Walsh (for young adults)*
  isbn 0-88878-219-5